Bradford Wilmer

Observations on the Poisonous Vegetables

which are either indigenous in Great Britain or cultivated for ornament

Bradford Wilmer

Observations on the Poisonous Vegetables
which are either indigenous in Great Britain or cultivated for ornament

ISBN/EAN: 9783337381189

Printed in Europe, USA, Canada, Australia, Japan

Cover: Foto ©Andreas Hilbeck / pixelio.de

More available books at **www.hansebooks.com**

T O

Sir WILLIAM WHELER, Bart.

THE FOLLOWING

O B S E R V A T I O N S

ON THE

VEGETABLE POISONS

OF

G R E A T - B R I T A I N,

ARE ADDRESSED,

By his moſt obedient, and

moſt humble Servant,

Coventry,
April 14, 1781.

BRADFORD WILMER.

PREFACE.

IN the vegetable world, the attentive obferver of nature hath for his contemplation a fcene, which is large and greatly varied. The mountain, the valley, the field, and the foreft, produce their peculiar plants; yet each of thefe fituations bears fuch as are of qualities oppofite to thofe of others that arife from the fame fpot of earth. United in the place from whence they derive their nourifhment, there is all imaginable diftance between their qualities : and whilft fome act with a kind influence upon the human frame, others undermine the fecret fupports of life. From the healing to the deftructive, there are many degrees in the fcale; yet numerous

as

as thefe gradations are, there probably may be found amongft our various vegetables thofe whofe virtues, or whofe baneful qualities, would fill up every rank.

Some botanical authors, in defcribing the powers of plants, feem to have been guided only by imagination. They afcribed to them qualities which nature never gave them, and fwelled beyond all probability thofe which they really poffefs. Almoft every plant which they treat of, would be a certain remedy for half the diforders in the world, or a moft fatal poifon, if the character they give to it were true. But experience is now believed, in frequent oppofition to Gerard and Parkinfon ; and many herbs which were celebrated by them for their medicinal virtues, no longer make

make a part of the materia medica;
whilft others are found perfectly innocent, which they had defcribed as
poifonous in their nature. It is hap-
py for men when they increafe their
knowledge by an obfervation of facts,
and no longer receive implicitly the
traditions of ignorant ages.

But it is ufual for thofe who find
they have been mifled, to give themfelves up too much to doubt. Thus
more than is true has been faid of
the virtues of plants, and now perhaps lefs than is true is believed. It
was found that the writings of bota-
nifts were largely fupplied with mif-
takes; and amidft the crowd of er-
rors which ftood ready to miflead
him, the unexperienced practitioner
did not know what he might fafely

truſt to.   He perceived in theſe
works that all was not to be credit-
ed, and therefore he almoſt rejected
all ; not recollecting that truth was
probably ſomewhere between the
two extremes.

I⊤ is fortunate that the number of
poiſonous herbs is very ſmall.   Even
of theſe the dreadful effects may be
prevented, by an immediate and proper attention, or removed, though
they have partly taken place.   They
appear to act by an impreſſion upon
the nervous ſyſtem, rather than by
an inflammation of the ſtomach and
duodenum, as mineral poiſons do,
which from this beginning produce
thoſe other intervening ſymptoms,
that uſually end in death.   In vain
would their offending ſubſtances be
removed from the ſtomach by emetics,

tics, if the diforder they occafioned there had arrived at a certain degree of violence.

Poisonous herbs in different con-ftitutions will have various and fome-times oppofite effects. This I fpeak from my own knowledge, having feen the moft contrary fymptoms produced in feveral perfons who had taken the fame poifon under equal circumftances. They exhibited a proof, that both the utmoft irrita-tion, and appearances which indi-cated that the office of the nerves was deftroyed, might arife from the fame caufe working its effects in dif-ferent conftitutions.

The vegetable poifons might per-haps be properly feparated into the two following divifions. The firft
. including

including thofe from which maniacal
fymptoms may be expected, or the
various nervous affections, from a
vertigo to a fatal apoplexy. Hither
might be referred the foporiferous
plants, which more flowly bring on
dangerous appearances, and are fel-
dom fatal in a fhorter fpace than
twenty-four hours, affording during
that time opportunities for the ufe
of emetics, the vegetable acids, and
proper ftimuli, which will generally
have the defired effect.

In the other clafs may be placed
fuch as produce epileptic fymptoms.
A lofs of underftanding, of fpeech,
and of all the fenfes, will take place
in a few minutes after thefe poifons
are in the ftomach: the mufcles will
be much convulfed, and death will
clofe

clofe the fcene in the fhort period of one hour or two.

THE danger of thefe poifons is very great. They do not offend the palate, and therefore may pafs unfuf-pected into the ftomach : when there, they ufually occafion no ficknefs, and therefore are not likely to be dif-charged without the affiftance of art : and they produce their effects fo haftily, that they fcarcely permit any opportunity for that affiftance to be given.

THERE are only three plants of this nature known in Great-Britain, two of which are natives of our ifland. They are the oenanthe crocata, cicuta aquatica, and lauro-cerafus. The laft is moft fatal, and requires a che-mical preparation. Its poifon may

therefore

therefore in fome meafure be faid to
be an invention of art.

SHOULD it be afked whether poifonous
plants have any ufe among the works
of nature, it might be replied, that in
judicious hands they become effectual
remedies for many complaints. They
are likewife innocent food to various
animals. Quails will thrive upon
hellebore, and goats upon water-
hemlock : ftarlings and other birds
feed upon the feeds of the cicuta
major. It might be added that there
are tribes of infects nourifhed and
protected by them, which ferve as a
prey to other creatures that are more
confiderable in the afcending climax
of the creation.

R E F E-

REFERENCES

EXPLAINED.

Bauhin. Pin.	CASPARI *Bauhini* Prodromus & Pinax. Bafil. 1671. 4to.
Bauhin. Hiſt.	Joannis *Bauhini* Hiſtoria Plantarum univerſalis. Ebrodunum. 1650. fol.
Columb. Ecph.	Fabii *Columnæ* Ecphraſis i. & ii. minus cognitarum, rariorumqueſtirpium. Romæ. 1616. 4to.
Cluſius.	Carolus *Cluſius,* in exoticorum libris.
Dodon. Pempt.	*Dodonæi* Pemptades. fol. 1616.
Flor. Scot.	Flora Scotica, by the Rev. John *Lightfoot,* 2 vol. 8vo. Lond. 1777.
Ger. Emac.	Joannis *Gerardi* Hiſtoria Plantarum à Thoma *Johnſon* Emaculata. Lond. 1633. fol.

G ſn.

Gefn. Hort.   *Gefnerus* de Hortis Germaniæ.

Hill.   *Hill's* Britifh Herbal. fol. London. 1756.

Haller. Helv.   Alberti *Haller* Hiftoria Stirpium indigenarum Helvetiæ. Bernæ. 1768. 2 vol. fol.

Hort. Eyſtet.   Bafilii *Beſleri* Hortus Eyſtettenſis. Noremb. 1613. fol.

Lin. Sp. Pl.   Caroli *Linnæi*, fpecies Plantarum. Holmiæ. 1762. 8vo. 2 vol.

Lob.   Lobelii Obfervationes Stirpium. fol. 1476.

Morif. Hiſt.   Roberti *Moriſoni* Hiftoria Plantarum Oxonienſis. 3 vol. fol. Oxon. 1680.

Morif. Umb.   Roberti *Moriſoni* Plantarum Umbelliferarum diſtributio nova. fol. Oxon. 1672.

Matthiol.   Petri *Matthioli* Commentaria Italica cum figuris. 1568. fol.

Miller.   *Miller's* Gardener's Dictionary.

Park.

Park.	Joannis *Parkinſoni* Theatrum Botanicum. fol. Lond. 1629.
Raii Syn.	Joannis *Raii* Synopſis Methodica Stirpium Britannicarum. 8vo. Lond. 1724.
Raii Hiſt.	*Ejuſdem* Hiſtoria Plantarum. 3 fol. 1704.
Storck.	Libellus de Stramonio, Hyoſciamo, & Aconito. Vindobonæ. 1762. 8vo. Libellus quo demonſtratur Cicutam, &c. Vindobonæ. 1760. 8vo.
Schwenck.	*Schwenckfeldius,* Catalogus Stirpium & Foſſilium Sileſiæ. Lipſiæ. 1601.
Tournef.	Joſephi Pitton *Tournefort* inſtitutiones Rei Herbariæ. Paris 1700. 4to.
Wepfer.	Cicutæ Aquaticæ Hiſtoria & Noxæ. Commentario illuſtrata. Joh. Jacobo *Wepfero.* Baſil. 1679. 4to.

C O N-

CONTENTS.

CLASS I.

OBSERVATIONS on hyoſcyamus niger.
Page 1.

Belladonna,	- - - -	14.
Napellus cœruleus,	- - -	26.
Cynocrambe,	- - - -	34.
Stramonium,	- - - -	37.
Cicuta major,	- - - -	42.
Agaricus muſcarius,	- - -	54.
Fungus piperatus,	- - -	57.

CLASS II.

Oenanthe crocata,	- - -	69.
Cicuta aquatica,	- - -	77.
Lauro-ceraſus,	- - - -	84.

OBSER-

OBSERVATIONS

ON

VEGETABLE POISONS.

CLASS I.

COMMON HENBANE.

HYOSCYAMUS foliis amplexicaulibus finuatis, floribus feffilibus. *Lin. Sp. Plant.* 257.

HYOSCYAMUS vulgaris & niger. *C. Bauhine*, Pin. 169.

HYOSCYAMUS niger. *Gerard. Hift. Pl.* 353.

THE root is long, tough, white, and when recently cut through, fmells like that of liquorice.

THE ftalks are thick, round, woody, irregularly branched, and covered with a hairy down.

THE

THE leaves furrounding the ftalk at their bafe, ftand irregularly. They are large, foft, and downy, pointed at the ends, and very deeply indented at the edges. Their colour is a greyifh green, and they have a virofe, difagreeable fmell.

THE flowers are monopetalous. They are numerous, fingular, divided into five obtufe fegments, and when accurately examined, are not without beauty, although they have an unpleafant appearance on the plant: they are large, of a dirty yellowifh colour, reticulated with violet-coloured veins.

THE feed-veffels follow one after every flower: they are large, and contain a great quantity of feeds: of a brown, rough, and irregular figure.

THIS is the only fpecies of henbane that is a native of Britain. It is common by road-fides and amongft rubbifh, and flowers in June.

DR. Withering obferves, that this plant is refufed by horfes, cows, fheep, and fwine *.

* Arrangement of Britifh Vegetables, vol. i. p. 119.

It

It appears to afford both protection and nu-
triment to fome infects; thefe are the chryfomela hyofcyami, and the fcarlet bug, *cimex
hyofcyami.*

HENBANE is a very dangerous poifon. The
feeds, leaves, and root, received into the human ftomach, are all poifonous. The root,
in a fuperior degree, produces fometimes
madnefs, and if taken in a large quantity,
and the ftomach does not reject it by vomiting, a ftupor and apoplectic fymptoms, terminating in death, are the ufual confequences.

HENBANE is frequently found upon dung-
hills, and its roots mixt with muck, are introduced into our gardens. In their external
appearance they much refemble thofe of
parfnep, from the ufe of which we often
hear of fatal effects; but it is very probable that the roots of henbane mixt with the
parfnep, which they much refemble, are the
unfufpected caufe of the mifchief.

My friend Mr. Harrold informs me that
he once faw two women, who from eating

the

the fuppofed roots of parfnep, became maniacal, and were fo furious, that ftrict con-
finement was neceffary for feveral days.

It has been afferted by medical authors of
great reputation *, that the roots of parfnep
continuing in the fame ground for fome years,
contract pernicious qualities, fo as to occafion
diforders of the fenfes. It appears, however,
inconfiftent with the fimple and uniform operations of nature to fuppofe that the root of
an wholefome and pleafant vegetable fhould
merely by continuing on the fame fpot, become noxious : it is furely much more reafonable to conclude, that the roots or feeds
of fome poifonous plant might be introduced
with manure, or by fome other means, into
the garden.

On the 10th of March, 1765, the family
of a farmer at Loughton in Buckinghamfhire,
confifting of fix perfons, dined upon pudding,
boiled meat, and the roots of parfnep. Soon
after dinner they all became ill, and in two

* Ray, Hiftoria Plantarum, i. 420. Dan. Hoffman,
acta acad. cæfar. nat. curiofor. vol. vi. anno 1742.
Obf. 128. p. 426.

hours

hours I was a witnefs of the following fcene.
—Mrs. York (the farmer's wife) was upon
a bed with all the fymptoms of an apoplexy.
Her pulfe was remarkably hard and full, her
face was red, the fenfes and voluntary motions were abolifhed; the refpiration was
difficult, and much opprefled. Two of the
children were ftupid, and appeared like thofe
intoxicated with fpirituous liquors. A man-
fervant and the maid, with uncommon agitation of mind, were dancing about the
room, with all the appearance of maniacal
perfons. A middle-aged man (the fhepherd)
had dined with the reft, and after dinner
went about his bufinefs in the fields. At
my requeft he was fought for, and brought
home by two men, who informed me that
they fortunately arrived time enough to prevent the poor man being drowned in a marl-
pit, near the banks of which he was ftagger-
ing like one (as they faid) dead drunk. I
attempted to give an active emetic to the
man-fervant, but as foon as he received it
into his mouth, he returned it into my face.
Five grains of emetic tartar, diffolved in
water, were conveyed into the ftomach, by
means of a funnel, and he foon vomited up

large

large quantities of the roots, &c. In a short time he recovered the ufe of his reafon, and complained of nothing more than a flight head-ach. An emetic was given to all the reft, except Mrs. York, and after the ftomach had rejected the contents, they recovered in a very fhort fpace of time.

Mrs. York had never eat any parfneps before in her life, but being prevailed upon, unfortunately, to tafte them, fhe took more than any one of the family. All attempts to convey medicine into her ftomach were ineffectual. Acrimonious and purgative glifters were injected, without producing any evacuation. The moft powerful ftimulants were applied to various parts of the body without any apparent effect; fhe could not be awakened by any methods that were put in practice for that purpofe. In the evening the apoplectic fnoring increafed, attended with a quick pulfe; her extremities were warm and moift with fweat. During the night, the difficulty of refpiration, was accompanied with a rattling in the bronchia; the noftrils were compreffed, her feet became cold, and at fix o'clock in the morning fhe died.

died. I could not obtain permiffion to open
the body.

Suspecting that the roots of fome poifonous plant were mixed with the parfneps,
I defired to fee fome of them. They
brought me a fpecimen from the garden,
and upon an accurate examination, I perceived them evidently of two kinds. As the
roots at that time were not furnifhed with
leaves, I took them home, and planted them
in a garden. Some of them proved to be
the paftinacha fativa, or garden parfnep, and
the other the hyofcyamus niger, or common henbane.

A specimen of the leaves of the plant,
and a defcription of the cafe, were tranfmitted to the Royal Seciety.

Many other well attefted inftances of the
pernicious effects of henbane have been recorded.

In the year 1729, a perfon came to con-
fult Sir Hans Sloane upon an accident that
happened to four of his children, aged from

B 4   four

four years and a half to thirteen years, by
their eating fome feeds they had gathered in
the fields, which they had miftaken for fil-
berts: by one of the capfules, Sir Hans
Sloane inftantly knew it to be that of the hyofcyamus niger vulgaris (or the common
henbane) which bears fome grofs refemblance
to the hufk of a filbert, and the feeds are
like thofe of the poppy. The fymptoms
that appeared in all the four were, great
thirft, giddinefs of the head, dimnefs of
fight, ravings, and profound fleep; which
laft in one of them continued two days and
two nights. Sir Hans ordered them all to
be bled, bliftered in feveral places, and afterward purged with a medicine compofed of
elect. linit. ol. amygd. dulc. flor. fulphur &.
fyr. flor. perfic. which operated both by vomit and ftool, and by this method they perfectly recovered *.

THE poifonous effects of henbane are now
fo well eftablifhed, that no doubt of the fact
can remain. In its operation and effects it

---

* Inftances of the violent operation of henbane are
given by Wepfer. De Cicuta Aquatica, p. 230, &c.

very

very much refembles thofe occafioned by opium when taken in large quantities; and like
opium alfo, in a proper dofe, and adminiftered with judgment and care, it may become a
very ufeful medicine in the hands of the
cautious practitioner.

PREPARATIONS of henbane are not only
fedative, eafing pain, and leffening morbid
irritability in a remarkable degree, but are
likewife exempt from an inconvenience which
always attends the ufe of opium. Opium
occafions coftivenefs, whereas the extract, or
other preparations of the hyofcyamus, are
obferved to keep the body regularly open.

DR. Storck evaporated the frefh expreffed
juice from the ftalks and leaves of this plant
over a gentle fire, to the confiftence of an
extract.

Two drachms of this extract were forced
down the ftomach of a middle fized dog.
Soon afterward he feemed timorous, and
lapped a great deal of water. In about half
an hour he fell into a languor, kept his eyes
open, and the pupils were very much dilated;

lated; he ftaggered as he walked, ftumbled againft every thing in his way, and appeared to have loft his fight. Then he laid himfelf to fleep, in which he difcovered anxiety; and the pit of his ftomach was often violently retracted. In about two hours he caft up all he had fwallowed, and when he ftood he trembled; and was very feeble.

AFTER vomiting three times, he had five ftools. The fœces were liquid, dufkifh, and very fetid. His eyes continued immovable, the pupil very much dilated, and his fight feemed to be almoft gone. Then he began to fleep again, the fpafms about the pit of the ftomach abated, and gradually went off. He flept four hours, and lay very ftill, nor did his limbs quiver as they had done a little time before. After this fleep his eyes returned to their natural ftate, and his fight feemed to be perfectly reftored : his ftrength was good; he was brifk, and fwallowed bread and flefh with a good appetite.

THIS dog was kept feveral weeks, in all which time he was healthy, watchful, and brifk.

DR.

Dr. Storck after this fwallowed every day during the fpace of a week one grain of the extract of henbane, without any inconvenience. He obferved that he had a better appetite, and his body was more foluble than ufual. Hence he concluded it might fafely, in fmall dofes, be adminiftered to his patients.

A woman 37 years of age, in the hofpital at Vienna, to which Dr. Storck was phyfician, had been for more than a year almoft every day afflicted with violent convulfions. The moft powerful antifpafmodics, which were either recommended by the beft authors, or which in fimilar cafes had been known to have been ferviceable, were adminiftered without any good effect. Opium only, in large dofes, fhortened the duration of the paroxyfms, lulled the pains, but never prevented a return : and it brought on a very obftinate and habitual coftivenefs. In this ftate of the cafe Dr. Storck gave every day, at intervals, three grains of extract of henbane.

In

In four days time she obferved her appetite to return, her body was more open, and the convulfive fits were much abated in their violence and continuance. She then was ordered to take fix grains of the extract. During feven fucceeding days she had no return of the convulfions, and enjoyed quiet and refrefhing fleep. On the eighth day she had fome flight twitchings in her legs and feet, but they did not continue long. During the two following months she took, each day, nine grains of the extract, but as no returns of the convulfions were perceived in that fpace of time, she forbore its farther ufe, and obtained a permanent cure.

Dr. Storck informs us that he afterwards adminiftered the extract of henbane in twelve other cafes, fome of which had obftinately refifted the moft efficacious medicines.

They were chiefly of the fpafmodic kind, and if his relation of them is to be depended on, they prove that henbane in guarded dofes is one of the moft powerful fedative medicines with which we have hitherto been acquainted, poffeffing the virtues of opium,

without

without occafioning the inconvenience which might arife from coftivenefs.

THE fmoke of henbane conveyed to the part, through a fmall tube, is faid to be a very certain cure for the tooth-ach.

THE leaves applied externally in the form of cataplafm, fomentation, or unguent, are difcutient, anodyne, and abate not only inflammatory but rheumatic pain *.

* Vide Lewis Mater. Med. p. 315. Lindeftolphe, de Venenis, cap. v. p. 552. Konig. Regnum Vegetab. p. 869. Hoyer, Act. phyfico-med. nat. curiof. vol. v. p. 260. Hoffman Phil. Corp. Human. cap. vii. Haller, Stirp. helvet. p. 513. Wepfer, de Cicut. Aquat. Hiftor. & Noxæ.

DEADLY

DEADLY NIGHTSHADE.

Belladonna. *Ray's Syn.* 265.

Solanum melano cerafus. *C. Bauhine.*

Atropa caule herbaceo, foliis ovatis integris. *Lin. Sp. Pl.* 260. *Gerard. Hift. Plant.* 340. *Moris. Hift.*

Solanum lethale. *Park.* 346.

THE root is long, large, and creeping.

THE ftalks are upright, firm, numerous branched, and herbaceous.

THE leaves are egg-fliaped, entire, very large, fmooth at the edges, pointed a little at the extremities, and of a beautiful green colour.

THE flowers ftand on fingle foot ftalks: they are formed of one petal; bell-fliaped, and very lightly divided into five fegments at the edge. Their colour is a dark dead purple.

THE

THE berries which fucceed the flowers are globular; they are firft of a red colour, and afterward become black. They have a tempting appearance, and from that circumftance many have been induced to eat them to their deftruction. It flowers in July.

THE deadly nightfhade is found in woods, hedges, and where the ground is rich from manure, in the neighbourhood of towns and houfes. It is a native of England.

LIGHTFOOT * found it in the king's park at Stirling and Icolumbkill.

THE whole plant is poifonous, and the berries † eaten by children, from their

---

* Flora Scotica, p. 142. vol. i.

† Buchanan, the Scotch hiftorian, defcribes the deftruction of the army of Sweno, when he invaded Scotland. It feems the Scots, by a truce, had engaged to fupply the army of their invader with drink, and in this they mixt the juice of the berries of deadly nightfhade. The Danes became fo intoxicated, that the Scots fell upon them in their fleep, and killed the greateft part of them; fo that there were fcarcely men enough left to remove the king in fafety. This account is probably fabulous.

beautiful

beautiful appearance, have often occafioned the moft fatal effects.

THE works of medical authors abound with inftances of the deleterious effects of the deadly nightfhade, and experience hath fufficiently afcertained the truth of their relations.

THIS plant has a faint fmell, fomewhat of the poppy kind, which is loft when it is dry; whether frefh or dry, there is no peculiar fenfation conveyed, when the leaves are applied to the organs of tafte.

MR. Ray informs us of a remarkable effect which a fmall part of the leaf of Belladonna had when applied to a fmall ulcer, which a lady was afflicted with beneath the eye. In one night the iris was fo much relaxed, that it became paralytic, and did not contract the pupil at the approach of the ftrongeft light. It was dilated to four times its natural fize, till the leaf being removed, the parts gradually recovered their tone.

THE

THE application was repeated three feveral times, and always produced the fame effect *.

DR. Hill † obferves, that he once faw an unhappy inftance of the fatal effects of this poifon.

IN the year 1743, a labourer found the berries of the deadly nightfhade in a nobleman's park, where he was repairing the pales. He gave fome of the berries to his children, and fwallowed a large quantity himfelf. The fymptoms came on in the following manner. The man after two hours became light-headed, giddy, and unable to ftand; but not thinking of the caufe, fat down to fupper. He drank greedily, but could fcarce fwallow any thing folid. He went to bed, and prefently grew worfe. He complained of a dreadful pain in the breaft, and difficulty of breathing. It was about five in the afternoon when he eat the berries. Thefe fymptoms came on between ten and eleven at night: and at twelve, feven hours from the

* Hift. Plant. p. 680.   † Brit. Herb. p. 329.

C   eating

eating them, he fell into the moſt dreadful ravings. Once in a quarter of an hour his ſenſes would return for a moment; but he relapſed immediately, and every time with more violence. During the intervals of reaſon, his breathing was difficult, and he complained of a dreadful tightneſs croſs his breaſt. Towards morning the ravings went off, but he became fooliſh. He was faint, breathed with difficulty, and ſtared and ſlabbered, anſwering foreign to queſtions, and ſeemed a perfeƈt idiot. All this time he was affeƈted with a moſt violent ſtrangury; but by degrees this went off, and he recovered without the help of medicines. Before the country apothecary could be had, he was growing better; and he not knowing what to adviſe, left the family to their own management. The children both died in the courſe of the night. The father, when perfeƈtly recovered, and queſtioned about the nature of the caſe, anſwered that he had been in the condition of one very drunk, but ſaw and underſtood all that was doing, even when he anſwered in the wildeſt manner.

THE

THE accounts given by other authors agree with the above defcription : and we read of men who have continued in a ftate of madnefs from nightfhade feveral days. To children it generally proves fatal. When adults die of this poifon, the fcene is ufually clofed within 24 hours *.

SOME boys and girls perceiving in a garden at Edinburgh the beautiful berries of the deadly nightfhade, and, unacquainted with their poifonous quality, eat feveral ; in a fhort time dangerous fymptoms appeared, a fwelling of the abdomen took place, they became convulfed : the next morning one of them

* Wepfer de Cicut. Aquat. p. 226. has given an account of fome dangerous fymptoms which affected three children from eating the berries of the folanum vulgare, common or garden nightfhade ; but as they all recovered, and as I have not met with an inftance where that fpecies of nightfhade proved fatal, I have on that account omited a defcription of it. Befides the folanum commune, there are other plants in this kingdom which are fufpected to be poifonous ; thefe are aconitum hyemale, colchicum vulgare, alkekengi multiflorum foliis hirfutis, fuppofed to be the folanum fomniferum of the ancients.

C 2   died,

died, and another in the evening of the fame
day, although all poffible care was taken of
them *.

On the twenty-fourth of September, 1771,
Dr. Lambert was defired to vifit two children
at Newburn in Scotland, who the preceding
day had fwallowed fome of the berries of the
deadly nightfhade. He found them in a de-
plorable fituation; the eldeft (10 years of
age) was delirious in bed, and affected with
convulfive fpafms. The younger was not
in a much better condition, in his mother's
arms. The eyes of both the children were
particularly affected. The whole circle of
the cornea appeared black, the iris being fo
much dilated as to leave no veftige of the
pupil. The tunica conjunctiva much inflamed. Thefe appearances, accompanied
with a remarkable kind of ftaring, exhibited
a very affecting fcene. The fymptoms came
on about two hours after they had eaten the
berries: they appeared at firft as if they had
been intoxicated, afterwards loft the power
of fpeaking, and continued the whole night

* Lond. Mag. Sept. 1747.

fo

fo unruly, that it was with much difficulty they were kept in bed.

DR. Lambert gave them 15 grains of white vitriol, which foon occafioned a ficknefs. The emetic was repeated, and they vomited plentifully; they were ordered to drink an oily emulfion. Cathartic medicines were given by the mouth, and a common clyfter was adminiftered. At twelve o'clock at night, the purgative medicines produced the wifhed-for effect, and the ftools appeared purple like the juice of the berries, intermixed with their black fkins: after this they were foon relieved: they fpoke, and became fenfible; but their eyes continued feveral days in a weak ftate, and the laft fymptom which remained was a vertigo.

IT appears from the hiftory of this cafe, that emetics were of no ufe, and the reafon is very obvious. Dr. Lambert was not called till twenty-one hours had elapfed from the time the children eat the berries, and the ftomach had probably long before paffed them into the inteftines.

C 3   THE

THE dangerous effects of the deadly night-shade were known to the ancients. Theoph:aftus called this plant ftrychnos, and the symptoms which it produced were called ftrychnomania. Subfequent authors have ventured to recommend the internal ufe of it in very fmall quantities in obftinate dif-eafes; and if we believe the teftimony of Mr. Ray *, the external application of the leaves in the form of a cataplafm, have been found efficacious in cancerous complaints. An in-fufion of the berries given internally has been faid to have been fuccefsful in inflam-mations †, and dyfenteries ‡. Juncker informs us, that two cancerous cafes were cured by it, and recommends its farther ufe §.

In the year 1754, Dr. Lambergen printed at Groningen an inaugural differtation, to which was added an account of a cancer in a woman's breaft, that had been radically cured by the infufion of the leaves of deadly night-shade. This cafe was publifhed eight years

---

* Ray's Hift. Plant. p. 680.
† Tragus, Stirp. Hift. p. 305.
‡ Ray's Hift. Pl. Lin. Mat. Med. § 95.
§ Confpect. Chirurg. p. 314.

after

after the cure was perfected, and the woman is faid to have continued perfectly well.

FROM reading this cafe, the late Mr. Gataker determined to try the effects of nightfhade in St. George's hofpital. He adminiftered it in a variety of cancerous cafes, as well as fcrophulous and fcorbutic ulcers, but his fuccefs was in the fequel by no means equal to the fanguine expectations he had formed of it. In the firft paper he communicated to the Royal Society upon this bufinefs, he gave an account of fome cafes wherein it appeared to have been attended with fuccefs. From the recommendation of Mr. Gataker, the folanum was alfo tried in moft of the public hofpitals of London. By the concurrent teftimony of feveral furgeons, under whofe infpection it was adminiftered, it was at length agreed, that the nightfhade was by no means poffeffed of any fpecific properties either againft cancerous or fcrophulous difeafes; that moft of the patients in whofe cafes it appeared at firft to be ferviceable, relapfed; that it was, except in fmall dozes, unmanageable in its effects; that it was extremely uncertain in the mode

C 4   of

of its operation, fometimes violently purging
the patient, fometimes ftimulating the kidneys, or increafing greatly the cuticular difcharge, and fometimes producing no evacuation of any kind; that, in fhort, no confequence of its adminiftration was with any
certainty to be expected, except the mifchief
it did to the organs of vifion. Moft of thofe
who took it complained either of giddinefs,
violent throbbing pain in the eyes, with a
difcharge of tears, and in all the pupil was
as much dilated, and had the fame appearance, as if the patient laboured under a con-
cuffion of the brain, or paralytic ftate of the
optic nerve : and it was much fufpected that
the ufe of the folanum haftened the death of
feveral who took it *.

Mr. Gataker, however, in a publication
fince the obfervations he communicated to
the Royal Society, ingenuoufly acknowledges,
that his expectations were not anfwered;
that the event of fome cafes difappointed his
firft hopes, either by the cure proving in-
complete, or only temporary; that he found

* Bromfield on Nightfhade, p. 69.

from

from further experience, the operation of the medicine to be irregular, and the ufe of it in fome inftances, if perfevered in, attended with troublefome fymptoms. He obferves alfo, that nightfhade is a medicine not fo much calculated for general ufe, as for particular cafes, where the common remedies have failed, and where this feems, *upon trial*, to be free from the principal inconveniences which fo often attend the ufe of it *.

* Gataker's Effays, p. 87.

BLUE

BLUE MONKSHOOD.

ACONITUM foliorum laciniis linearibus, fuperne latioribus, linea exaratis. *Lin. Spec.*
Pl. p. 538.

ACONITUM cæruleum, five Napellus. *J.*
Bauhine.

Napellus verus. *Lobel.*

ACONITUM fpica florum pyramidali. *Morif.*

THE root is divided into feveral parts :
it is long, thick, and has many
fibres.

THE leaves rife from the root very early
in the fpring: they appear firft in a globular form, and when they expand, become
large, of a beautiful green colour, and are
divided into numerous, long, narrow fegments. This plant is four feet high. The
leaves from the ftalk are placed irregularly,
they are fmaller than thofe which immediately arife from the root, but like them they
are fubdivided into numerous fegments.

THE

THE flower is extremely fingular; it has five petals, one of them is uppermoft, and is hooded, two are placed on the fides, and two below: the lateral petals are broad, and incline to each other; the inferior ones are longer than thofe on the fide, and droop downward. Within the flower are two nectaria. The flowers ftand on long fpikes, on the fuperior part of the branches; they are large, and of a full beautiful blue. Three capfules, inclofing the feeds, fucceed every flower.

BLUE Monkfhood is fpontaneoufly produced in Germany, and fome other northern parts of Europe, and is very common in our gardens, where it is cultivated for ornament.

THIS is certainly a poifonous plant, and many inftances have been adduced of its dangerous effects. Dodonæus gives an account of five perfons who eat the root of blue monkfhood in their food at Antwerp, and they all died. It has probably obtained the name of wolf's-bane from a tradition that wolves, in fearching for particular roots which they in part fubfift upon in winter, frequently

frequently make a miftake and eat the roots of napellus ceruleus, which generally proves fatal to them.

In the year 1764, John Crumpler, a weaver in Spitalfields, having fupped upon fome cold meat and fallad, was fuddenly taken ill; and when Mr. Bacon, the Surgeon employed upon this occafion, vifited him, he found him in the following fituation. He was in bed, with his head fupported by an affiftant, his eyes and teeth were fixed, his noftrils compreffed; his hands, feet, and forehead cold; no pulfe to be perceived; his refpiration fhort, interrupted, and laborious.

Mr. Bacon was informed, that foon after his patient had fupped, he complained of a fenfation of heat, affecting the tongue and fauces : his teeth appeared loofe; and it was very remarkable, although a looking-glafs was produced, and his friends attempted to reafon him out of the extravagant idea, yet he imagined that his face was fwelled to twice its ufual fize. By degrees the heat, which at fiift only feemed to affect the mouth and adjacent parts, diffufed itfelf over his body

and

and extremities; he had an unſteadineſs and laſſitude in his joints, particularly of the knees and ancles, with an irritable twitching of the tendons, which ſeemed to deprive him of the power of walking; and he thought that in all his limbs he perceived an evident inter- ruption to the circulation of the blood. A giddineſs was the next ſymptom, which was not accompanied with a nauſea. His eyes became watery, and he could not ſee diſ- tinctly : a kind of humming noiſe in his ears continually diſturbed him, until he was re- duced to the ſtate of inſenſibility before de- ſcribed.

BEFORE Mr. Bacon's arrival, ſome of his friends, believing he had been poiſoned, had forced down ſome oil and water, and after- ward ſome carduus tea, in conſequence of which, the ſtomach threw up its contents; but notwithſtanding this precaution, the ſymptoms increaſed.

MR. Bacon, by the repetition of carduus tea, &c. encouraged the vomiting, and in the intervals adminiſtered ſome ſpoonfuls of a ſtimulating cordial medicine. After ſome

time

time the patient feemed relieved, and by degrees recovered.

Mr. Bacon was informed that the fallad which the patient had eaten for fupper, con- fifted of common herbs bought at a ftall in the market, except fome celery picked out of their own garden. He defired to fee fome of the celery: a fpecimen was brought to him, which Mr. Bacon perceived was the blue Monkfhood, or aconitum cæruleum.

Dr. Storck, of Vienna, reduced to powder the leaves and ftalks of blue monkfhood: fome of this applied to his tongue, occafioned fome tranfient, although pungent pains in his mouth, accompanied with a fenfation of heat. With a view to afcertain whether the powder had any corrofive effects, he fprinkled fome of it upon the furface of a fungous ul- cer. The patient complained neither of heat nor pain; and although the application was feveral times renewed, the fungous flefh was neither confumed nor reftrained in its progrefs. Dr. Storck after this evaporated the expreffed juice to the confiftence of an extract. Some of this applied upon the

tongue,

tongue, occafioned a flight titillation. He infinuated a grain of the extract between his eye-lids, without obferving the effects of any preternatural irritation. He afterwards prepared the following powder:

 ℞ Extract. Napel. cærul. gr. ii.

  Sach. puris. ʒ ii. M. & contrite in mortario marmoreo.

THE Doctor took ten grains of this powder without any apparent operation. He then fwallowed twenty grains. Throughout the whole day, a very profufe perfpiration was the confequence. Hence he inferred, that as the extract of monkfhood increafed fo very remarkably the cuticular difcharge, it was adapted to difeafes in which the morbid matter might be expelled by the fudoriferous pores.

DR. Storck and Dr. Colin, we are informed, adminiftered the extract of monkfhood to fourteen different patients in the hofpital at Vienna, with aftonifhing fuccefs. It relieved in a fhort time the violent pains of the gout and chronic rheumatifm, by occafioning a plentiful diaphorefis; it foftened and even
        diffolved

diſſolved chalk-ſtones, nodes, tophi, and
cured exoſtoſes. Unfortunately however it
happens, that experiments made upon the
napellus in this country, do not confirm all
that has been ſaid of it by Dr. Storck. I
evaporated the juice expreſſed from the
leaves and ſtalks of blue monkſhood to the
conſiſtence of an extract. I tried it with
two patients who had the chronic rheuma-
tiſm, and it was adminiſtered in the doſes
recommended by Dr. Storck. After having
given it (what I thought) a fair trial, and
finding it do neither good or harm, I threw it
aſide for the uſe of more efficacious remedies.

THE napellus is ſaid by authors not to be
poiſonous in Sweden and ſome other coun-
tries. In the Ephemer. Medic. Phyſ. Curioſ.
An. 11. Obſ. 42. p. 79. is a treatiſe under
the following title : D. Martini Barnardi à
Bernz. Napellus in Polonia non venenoſus,
wherein ſome inſtances are given to prove
that the napellus mentioned by Linnæus is
not poiſonous in Poland.

IT muſt be obſerved, however, that the
kind of napellus mentioned by Linnæus not

to

to be poifonous in Sweden, is not the blue monkfhood, but the aconitum lycoctonum luteum majus. Bauhin. or yellow monkfhood, which Linnæus faw a family in Sweden mix and eat with their foup, without any bad confequences.

LIGHTFOOT * found this plant in Scotland, in feveral places, about Hoddamcaftle, in Annandale, &c. but always near houfes, fo that he fufpected it was not indigenous.

* Flor. Scot. vol. i. p. 485.

DOGS

DOGS MERCURY.

Mercurialis caule fimpliciffimo, foliis fcabris.
Lin. Sp. Plant. 1465. (*Gerard.* 333. f. 1.
Pet. Herb. t. i. f. 5 & 6.   *Moris. Hift.* f.
5. t. 34. f. 3 & 4.)

Mercurialis perennius repens Cynocrambe
dicta.   *Ray's Syn.* 138.

Cynocrambe mas & fœmina.   *Gerard.* 333.

Mercurialis montana fpicata.   *Bauh. Pin.*
122.

Mercurialis fylveftris Cynocrambe dicta vulgaris, mas & fœmina.   *Park.* 295.

THE root is creeping, light-coloured,
and fibrous.

THE ftalk is a foot high, erect, green,
juicy, and unbranched.

THE leaves are oval, ferrated, pointed at
the extremity, placed in pairs oppofite to
each other.

THE

THE flowers grow at the tops of the ftalk, and in thin flender fpikes out of the alæ of the leaves, and are of a light green. The flowers are of two kinds, male and female. The furrows of the *germen* receive a barren filament, terminated with a gland, marked with two dark-coloured fpots.

IT is found very common in woods, fhady places, upon ditch banks, and flowers very early in fpring.

LIGHTFOOT * found it in many parts of Scotland, both in the Highlands and Low-lands.

THIS plant is poifonous. It is of a fopo-rific deleterious nature, and is faid to be noxious both to man and beaft. Many in-ftances are recorded of its fatal effects.

MR. Ray acquaints us with the cafe of a man, his wife, and three children, who were poifoned by eating the cynocrambe fried with bacon.

* Flor. Scot. vol. ii. p. 621.

D 2   A

A melancholy inftance is related in the Philofophical Tranfactions, N° CCIII. of its pernicious effects upon a family who eat at fupper the herb boiled and fried. It produced at firft naufea and vomiting, and afterwards comatofe fymptoms. Two of the children flept twenty-four hours: when they awakened, they vomited again and recovered. The other girl could not be awakened during four days, at the expiration of which time fhe opened her eyes and expired.

Dr. Withering * obferves, that the cynocrambe is eaten by goats and fheep, and refufed by cows and horfes. When it is infufed in water, it affords a fine deep blue colour. Lightfoot † fays it is called in the ifle of Skye, lus-glen-bracadale; and that he was there informed, it is fometimes ufed in a weak infufion to bring on a falivation. The experiment, however, feems dangerous.

* Arrangement of Britifh Vegetables, vol. ii. p. 616.
† Flor. Scot. vol. ii. p. 621.

THORN-

THORN-APPLE.

DATURA pericarpiis fpinofis, erectis ovatis. *Lin. Sp. Pl.* p. 179.

SOLANUM fœtidum, pomo fpinofo oblongo, flore albo infundibuli formi. *C. Bauh. Pin.* p. 168.

SOLANUM maniacum. *Diafcor. Colum.*

SOLANUM pomo fpinofo oblongo, flore cala-thoide, ftramonium vulgo dictum. *Ray's Syn.* 266.

STRAMONIUM fpinofum. *Gerard.* 349.

THE root is long, large, and fibrous.

THE ftalk is of a pale green, ftrong, and near three feet high.

THE leaves are large, of a lively green, placed on ftrong peduncles; they are broad, pointed at the extremity, beautifully indent-ed, and are placed without any regular ar-rangement.

THE flower confifts of one petal, funnel-
fhaped, tubular, and folded at the border in
five parts. They grow at the bifurcations
of the branches, are large, and of a milk-
white colour.

THE feed-veffel is oval, large, and covered
with fhort, fharp, ftrong thorns. The feeds
are brown. It flowers in Auguft.

IT is a native of South-America, and is
cultivated in our gardens either for its fin-
gularity or ornament.

DR. Withering fays, that cows, goats,
fheep, and horfes refufe it *. He likewife
acquaints us, that it is found common amongft
ubbifh, in the neighbourhood of London.

I HAVE likewife obferved the ftramonium
flourifh upon a bank on the London road
near Coventry; but it is probable the feeds
may have been conveyed thither from a large
nurfery-garden in the neighbourhood, and
where many foreign plants have been propagated. It is certain that the plant is not in-

* Arrangement of Englifh Veg. vol. i. p. 119.

digenous

digenous in this kingdom, nor did Mr. Lightfoot meet with it in Scotland.

THE seed-veffels of thorn-apple fupply nourifhment to many infects; and it is very common to fee the cup quite a fkeleton, the flefhy parts having been eaten away.

THE feeds and leaves of thorn-apple received into the human ftomach, produce firft a vertigo, and afterwards madnefs. If the quantity is large, and vomiting is not occafioned, it will undoubtedly prove fatal.

BOERHAAVE * informs us, that fome boys eating fome feeds of thorn-apple, which were thrown out of a garden, were feized with giddinefs, horrible imaginations, terrors, and delirium. Thofe that did not foon vomit, died.

THE plant has a difagreeable, naufeous fmell, when rubbed between the fingers.

DR. Storck expreffed the juice from the leaves and ftalks of thorn-apple in a marble

* Acad. Lect. on the Nerves, publifhed by Dr. Van Eems.

D 3   mortar,

mortar, and afterward evaporated it to the
confiftence of an extract.   He affifted in the
procefs, from whence his head feemed much
affected.   He placed a grain and a half of
the extract upon his tongue, and fuffered it
to diffolve.   Although it produced a very
naufeous tafte, he fwallowed it. It occafioned
no particular effects, and thence he concluded
it might, at leaft with fafety, be given to
patients. In looking over the writings of
medicinal authors, he found they all agreed
in the affertion, that thorn-apple difordered
the mind, caufed madnefs, and convulfions.
By the introduction, however, of a new mode
of reafoning, the Doctor made the following
inference: that, as thorn-apple, by diforder-
ing the mind, caufed madnefs in found perfons, it was probable, by difturbing and
changing the ideas and common fenfory, it
might bring the infane, and perfons deprived
of reafon, to a found ftate of mind : and by
a contrary motion, remove convulfions in the
convulfed.

DR. Storck, from this theory, proceeded
to practice in the hofpital at Vienna, and
publifhed feveral cafes wherein extract of
thorn-

thorn-apple, given in fmall dofes, and continued a long time, produced a cure. They
were maniacal and epileptic patients, who
the Doctor fays experienced the good effects
of this mode of treatment.

THE extract of thorn-apple, I believe, has
not been tried in England, at leaft to my
knowledge; and the reafon probably has
been, that we have been much difappointed
in what Dr. Storck has faid relative to the
medical effects of cicuta, and other poifonous
plants.

COMMON

COMMON HEMLOCK.

CONIUM, feminibus ftriatis. *Lin. Sp. Pl.* 349.

CICUTA. *Gerard.* 1061. *Ray's Syn.* 215.

CICUTA major. *Bauh. Pin.* 160. *Morif. Hift. Pl,* vol. iii. 290.

CICUTA vulgaris major. *Park.* 933.

CICUTA vulgaris. *Phyt. Brit.* 27. *Hill. Brit. Herb.* 411.

CICUTA major vulgaris maculata fœtens. *Storck de Cicut.*

CONIUM feminabus ftriatis foliolis tenuoribus. *Miller. Gard. Dict.*

THE root is white, perpendicular, and furnifhed with lateral fibres.

THE leaves, which early in the fpring arife from the root, are of a very dark green colour: they are minutely divided and fubdivided, and ferrated at the edges.

THE

THE ſtalk is fiſtulous, firm, upright, articulated, ſmooth, round, and ſix feet high: it is thickly ſtained with innumerable purple ſpots, of various ſizes, and indeterminate figures.

THE leaves are placed irregularly on the ſtalk; they are, like the radical ones, minutely interſected, and of a ſtrong green colour.

THE flowers are ſmall and white; each is compoſed of five petals, inflected, and heart-faſhioned. They are diſpoſed in large umbels, upon divided and ſubdivided branches.

THE ſeeds are rounded, ſtriated on one ſide, and plain on the other, and are of a brown colour.

HEMLOCK flowers in July, and is very common under hedges in moſt parts of Europe. Where the ſoil is rich and moiſt, it is obſerved to be more luxuriant than in other places.

THIS plant has a viroſe, diſagreeable ſmell, but the freſh juice communicates no particular impreſſion to the organs of taſte.

IF

IF the exprefled juice is placed in a ftate of reft until the feces fubfide, and afterward poured off, it feems to lofe all the fpecific flavour of the plant.

HEMLOCK received into the human fto-mach, has occafioned death; but, like other plants of the poifonous kind, it is not only innoxious to certain animals, but appears to furnifh them with food and nourifhment.

MR. Ray informs us, that he found the crop of a thrufh full of the feeds of hemlock, at a time when corn was plentiful *.

DR. Withering obferves, that hemlock is eaten by fheep, and refufed by horfes, cows, and goats. †.

LIKE other plants of the narcotick kind, the deleterious effects of hemlock are much leffened by vegetable acids ‡.

ALTHOUGH

* Nos quoque ventriculum otidis feu turdæ avis dif-fectum cicutæ femine refertum invenimus, quatuor tantum aut quinque frumenti granis intermixtis: quod etiam meffis tempore avis illa pro cicuta neglexerat: adeo delectatur cicuta. Hift. Plantar. vol. i. p. 451.

† Arrangement of Englifh Veg. vol. i. p. 163.

‡ Cicuta, præfens illud venenum, fi coquitur in ace-to, fine noxa comedi poteft, quod probavi aliquoties, experimenti

ALTHOUGH the root of hemlock has by many been fuppofed to be the moft active, and the moft poifonous part of the plant; yet it has been given in dofes of thirty grains in quartan agues, acute fevers *, and fchirrous livers †, without any ill effect.

MR. Ray informs us, that his friend Mr. Pettiver eat half an ounce of the root of this plant; and that Mr. Henley, a friend of Mr. Pettiver's, in his prefence eat, without any inconvenience, three or four ounces of the fame root §.

FROM thefe inftances, and many others, the poifonous effects of this plant have been much fufpected.

SINCE the cicuta was recommended by Dr. Storck as a certain cure for many of the

experimenti ergo, Lugduni Batavorum, ubi in foffis extra urbem frequens crefcit. Lindeftolpe, de Venenis, p. 431.

* Bowle apud Raium Hift. Plant. i. 451.

† Renealme, Obferv. iii. and iv. Etmuller, Schræder. Diluc. par. i. fect. ii. p. ш1.

§ Synopf. ed. 2. p. 326.

moft

moſt terrible complaints to which the human
body is ſubject, it has been in common uſe
in every part of Europe; and when we con-
ſider the great extent, and almoſt univerſality
of its application, in every chronic diſeaſe
which had withſtood the operation of other
remedies, it appears ſurpriſing that we have
not heard of a ſingle inſtance of its poiſonous
effects.   It has been given by the regular
phyſician, as well as the apothecary's appren-
tice, in large doſes, in the forms of extract,
powder, juice; and it has been applied externally in cataplaſms, fomentations, baths,
and injections. It has been very liberally adminiſtered to men, women, and children, with
impunity.   Either our hemlock muſt be
milder than that deſcribed by authors, or,
which is much more probable, quite a different plant.

CARDANUS * mentions a man who was
killed by eating a cake wherein hemlock was
an ingredient : and Braſſavola aſſures us, that
it is mortal not only to men, but alſo to geeſe
and ſwine. Inſtances of the deleterious effects

* Phil. Tranſ. N° 473.

of

of hemlock may be found in many other authors *.

IT is now generally underſtood that the
Athenian poiſon (cicuta †), of which So-
crates periſhed, was certainly not the plant
we call hemlock. It muſt either have been
the cicuta aquatica, or the oenanthe, ſuceo
viroſo.

SOME have imagined; particularly Dr.
Mead, that the celebrated poiſon of Athens,
with which condemned criminals were put
to death, was a compoſition ‡.

IT is anciently recorded of the people of
Marſeilles, that they had a poiſon kept by
the public, in which cicuta was only an ingredient; a doſe of which was allowed by
the magiſtrates to any one who could ſhew a
reaſon why he ſhould deſire death. This
very ſingular cuſtom, Valerius Maximus ob-
ſerves, came from Greece, particularly from

* Matthiolus, Scaliger, Kircher, Boccone, &c.

† Cicuta quoque venenum eſt, publica Athenienſium
pœna inviſa. Plin. 26, 13.

‡ Mead's Works, 4to Edit. p. 111.

the

the ifland Ceos, where he faw an example of it *.

THEOPHRASTUS fays, that Thrafyas, a great phyfician; had invented a compofition, which would caufe death without any pain; and that this was prepared with the juice of hemlock and poppy together, and did the bufinefs in a fmall dofe †.

THE cicuta major was called conium by Diofcorides and Theophraftus. Linnæus has expreffed his doubts with regard to the poi-fonous effects of this plant, and has retained the old name conium. Contradiction and confufion appear in the various accounts which authors give us of hemlock: and many accidents *faid* to have been the effects of cicuta, were certainly produced by water hemlock, or the oenanthe crocata. It appears extremely abfurd, that the fame name fhould be applied to two plants, which have fo little refemblance to each other, as the cicuta ma-jor, and cicuta aquatica. They bear their

* Valer. Max. lib. ii. c. 6. §. 8.
† Hift. Plant. lib. ix. c. 17.

flowers

flowers in umbels, and this is the chief circumftance in which they agree.

LUCRETIUS by cicuta certainly means water hemlock, when he informs us, that goats eat it freely; thofe animals have often been obferved to feed upon the cicuta aquatica, and it is very well known that hunger itfelf will not prompt them to touch the cicuta major *.

TORRENTIUS obferves, that Perfius has confounded cicuta with hellebore, or fome other certain cure for madnefs †.

THE ftalk of hemlock being hollow, light, and jointed : hence the poets often ufe its name for the reed, of which pipes were made ‡.

* —————— " pinguefcere fæpe cicuta
Barbigeros pecudes, homini quæ eft acre venenum."
LUCRETIUS.

† " Calido fub pectore mafcula bilis intumuit,
" Quam non extinxerit una cicuta." PERSIUS.

‡ " Et Zephyri cava per calamorum fibila primum.
" Agreftes docuere cavas inftare cicutas." LUCRET.

" Eft mihi difparibus feptem compacta cicutas fiftula."
VIRG. ECL. ii. 36.

E   THE

THE only well-attefted cafe of the poifonous effects of the cicuta major in England,
is the following :

DURING the rebellion in 1745, fome
Dutch troops were quartered at Waltham-
abbey, in Effex. On Sunday, May 6, two
of the foldiers collected in the fields, adjoin-
ing to that town, a quantity of herbs fufficient for themfelves and two others for dinner, when boiled with bacon. Thefe herbs
were accordingly dreffed, and the poor men
firft eat of the broth with bread, and afterwards the herbs with the bacon. In a fhort
time they were all feized with violent verti-
gos : foon after they were comatofe : two of
them became convulfed, and died in about
three hours. The people of the town were
much alarmed at this accident ; and Dr. Bar-
rowby, a phyfician, being upon the fpot,
immediately attended, and ordered the other
two, at that time almoft dead, large quantities of oil, by which means they threw up
moft of what they had eaten, and afterwards
became better. In all of them, the effects
refembled thofe produced by a large dofe of
opium.

THE

THE next day Dr. Watfon was at Wal-
tham-abbey, and faw one of the men fo
much recovered, that he only complained of
a heavinefs in his head; and the other was
fo well, as to be able to perform his regi-
mental exercifes. There was a fifth foldier,
who informed the doctor, that he eat fome
of the bread out of the broth, but perceived
very little inconvenience from it. It happened that the two men who gathered the
herbs were thofe that died.

A DUTCH officer attended Dr. Watfon to
an inn where there were two other foldiers,
who had feen and known the herbs which
had been eaten. He alfo attended the doctor
into the fields to fhew the plants growing.
They firft gathered the cicutaria vulgaris of
J. Bauhine, or cow-weed: then the myrrhis
fylveftris, feminibus afperis, of Cafper Bauhine, or fmall hemlock chervil. They then
gave the Doctor fome cicuta major, and
fmelling it, immediately faid, that was the
herb which killed their comrades; which
there was no reafon to doubt of, as the two
former plants grow under almoft every hedge,
and are eaten by cows, and given to tame

rabbits

rabbits for food; whereas cattle conftantly refufe to eat hemlock *.

THE reputation of hemlock, as a medicine, feems to be in a lofing ftate. In confequence of too much having been faid of its virtues, when it was firft introduced into practice, two little may perhaps now be believed: and becaufe it will not cure cancers, it is fuppofed by fome practitioners to be ineffectual in every difeafe whatever. As far as can be deduced from the different cafes in which it has been tried in England, hemlock poffeffes very confiderable medical virtues; and it has been proved to be deobftruent, and anodyne. It has been ferviceable in fcrophulous cafes. In painful ulcers, difcharging an ichourous lymph, the internal ufe of this plant has been known to procure eafe, to mend the difcharge, and improve the complexion of the fore. Whether thefe effects are obtained by any fpecific alteration of the fluids, or are merely produced by the fedative properties of cicuta, we are not certain. It is probable, however, it acts in this refpect by eafing

* Phil. Tranf. N° 471. p. 21.

pain.

pain. Hemlock, like opium, leſſens morbid irritability in a very remarkable degree, but, like opium, it does not occaſion coſtivenefs.

FONTANUS * affures us, that a patient recovering from the plague, and being unable to get any ſleep, had recourſe to cicuta with good effect. The remedy after ſome time was difcontinued, and in a fubfequent illnefs, endeavours were ufed to procure reſt by repeated dofes of opium, which had no operation; and the ufe of cicuta was again called in with the defired fuccefs.

WE frequently hear of people being fuddenly taken ill after eating muſhrooms; and inſtances are recorded of their fatal effects. It is to be lamented, that upon thefe occaſions the particular ſpecies of fungus is ſeldom afcertained. Dr. Percival, in the laſt volume of his eſſays, page 267, relates the cafe of a man who was poifoned by eating a muſhroom, which Mr. Hudfon thinks was the fungus parvus, pediculo oblongo, of Ray. In the very numerous claſs of fungi, which Great-Britain produces, the agaricus mufcarius, and the fungus piperatus, may be reckoned the moſt poifonous.

* Nic. Fontani Refponf. & Curat. Medic. p. 162.

BUG

BUG AGARIC.

Agaricus Mufcarius.

Agaricus ftipitatus, lamellis dimidiatis fo-
litariis, ftipite volvato, apice dilatato, bafi
ovato. *Lin. Sp. Plant.* 1640.

Fungus minor campeftris rotundus, lamel-
latus, inferne albus, fuperne purpureus.
Ray's Synopf. 3.

THE pillar or ftalk is white, thick,
and hollow; egg-fhaped at the bafe,
and furrounded at the middle with a pendu-
lous membrane.

THE pileus, or hat, is large, almoft flat,
fix inches or more in diameter, of a red or
crimfon colour, fometimes befet with angu-
lar, white, downy warts.

THE lamellæ, or gills, are white, flat, and
inverfely fpear-fhaped : the greater number
extend from the rim of the pileus to the
ftalk, the reft only half way.

WHEN

WHEN the fungus is decaying, the gills become of a brownifh complexion.

IN Scotland this and other fungi of the agaric kind, are called paddock-ftools. It grows in woods, and frequently in paftures.

LIGHTFOOT obferved it in Scotland, at Blair in Athol, and in the woods at the cafcades of Monefs, near Taymouth *.

THE agaricus mufcarius will deftroy bugs, if rubbed upon the parts of the bed, where they retreat in the day. The inhabitants in the north of Europe, whofe houfes at the end of fummer are infefted with flies, infufe it in milk, and fet it in their windows. As foon as the flies tafte it, they are inftantly . poifoned.

HALLER relates, that fix perfons of Lithuania, in Poland, perifned at one time by eating it; and that in Kamtfchatka it had driven others raving mad. Two or three of thefe fungi may perhaps be eaten without

* See Lightfoot's Flora Scotica, vol. ii. p. 1010.

E 4   danger,

danger, but more will intoxicate, and bring on a delirium. The Ruffians, however, are bold enough to eat thefe, and almoft every other kind of fungus. Perhaps they are pleafed with their inebriating quality; for in the *natural* hiftory of Kamtfchatka, (p. 208, 209) we are told that the inhabitants prepare a liquor from an infufion of this agaric and the epilobium anguftifolium, which taken in a fmall quantity exhilarates the fpirits, but in a larger dofe brings on a trembling of the nerves, intoxication, delirium, and mad-nefs *.

* Flor. Scot. vol. ii. p. 1010.

PEPPER

PEPPER AGARIC.

FUNGUS piperatus albus, lacteo fucco turgens. *Ray's Synopf.* 4.

FUNGUS albus acris. *Bauh. Pin.* 370.

AGARICUS ftipitatus, pileo planiufculo lactefcente, margine deflexo, lamellis incarnato-pallidis. *Lin. Sp. Pl.* 1641.

T H E ftalk is about two inches high.

THE pileus is convex when young: as it expands, it becomes nearly flat: its colour is a dirty white, with a mixture of grey.

THE difk is conftantly bent inwards: when the fungus is decaying, the hat becomes depreffed in its centre, and is fometimes feen funnel-fhaped.

THE lamellæ are clofe, numerous, and of a pale frefh colour. When any part of this fungus is wounded, a cream-coloured liquid diftils from the part, extremely acrid

in

in its nature, and very ftimulating if applied
to the tongue.

It is very common in woods, particularly
near the roots of trees. Lightfoot obferved
it at Blair in Athol, and many other places
in Scotland *.

This fungus, when freely taken, has
been attended with fatal confequences †.
John Bauhine informs us, that after having
handled it, he rubbed his eyes by accident,
and brought on a violent irritation upon the
eye-lids : and it is remarkable, that when
this vegetable has loft its acrid juice by ex-
ficcation, its cauftic quality remains.

The deleterious effects of fome of the
fungi were known to the ancients, particularly the boletus, mentioned by Juvenal, on
account of the death of the emperor Claudius ‡.
This circumftance is alfo defcribed by Pliny.

SOME

* Flor. Scot. vol. ii. p. 1014.

† Vide J. and C. Bauhine, Ray, Morifon, Tourne-
fort, Vaillant, Dillenius, and Micheli, who have given
inftances of the pernicious effects of fungi.

‡ " Vilibus ancipites fungi ponentur amicis
   " Boletus domino, fed qualem Claudius edit.
   " Ante illum uxoris, poft quem nil amplius edit."
                                        SAT. v.
                              " —— Minus

SOME fpecies of the boletus are now eaten in Italy, when young, and are efteemed a great delicacy. The Germans alfo receive them as a dainty under the name of gombas and brat-biilz.

MR. Lightfoot obferves that deer, fheep, and fwine will feed upon the boleti, and are fometimes difordered by them. In cows and other cattle they have been known to create bloody urine, naufeous milk, fwellings of the abdomen, inflammation in the bowels, diarrhœas, and death. It is from hence obvious how cautious men ought to be in the ufe of them.

SCARABS, dermeftes, and many other infects feed upon and breed in them in abundance, and doubtlefs it is their proper food. It is pity men fhould rob them of it.

THE effects of the noxious fungi cannot be better defcribed than in the words of the celebrated Haller.

" —— Minus ergo nocens erit Agrippinæ
" Boletus: fiquidem unius præcordia preffit
" Ille fenis, tremulumque caput defcendere juffit
' In cœlum. SAT. vi,

" ALL

" All fungi are crude in their nature, of
" fpeedy growth, and fudden decay. They
" fpring up, arrive at maturity, and perifh in
" a few days, moft of them diffolving away
" in a black corrupted liquor, of a fœtid
" naufeous fmell. They are the food of
" fnails, beetles, flies, maggots, and the
" nidus where they depofit their young.

" The Ruffians, indeed, devour almoft
" every fpecies, even thofe which other na-
" tions efteem the moft poifonous, fuch as
" the agaricus mufcarius, piperatus, &c. but
" all of them are a doubtful and fufpicious
" food, and the moft innocent have proved
" fometimes prejudicial.

" By analyfis, it is found that feven parts
" of eight in their compofition are watery.
" They yield, by fire, a yellow fpirit like
" hartfhorn, a yellow empyreumatic oil,
" and a dry, volatile, chriftalline falt: fo
" that their nature is evidently alkaline, ex-
" tremely prone to corruption.

" Their fibres are tough, and very diffi-
" cult to digeft, fwelling in the ftomach like
" a

" a fponge : and there are inftances of their
" remaining undigefted for three days, be-
" fore their bad effects have appeared. The
" maladies they occafion are a fwelling of
" the abdomen, reftleffnefs, heart-burns,
" vomitings, colics, difficulty of refpiration,
" hiccoughs, melancholy, diarrhœas, accom-
" panied with a tenefmus, and gangrenes.
" To which dreadful complaints, the acri-
" monious quality of fome fungi bring on
" befides, inflammations in the mouth,
" with dyfenteric ftools.

" LASTLY, it is certain that fome fpecies
" have an intoxicating quality, followed
" often by deliria, tremblings, watchings,
" faintings, apoplexies, cold fweats, and
" death itfelf.

" SOME have fancied that fkilful cookery
" would deprive them of their bad effects,
" and that oils would fheath their noxious
" qualities ; but thefe are fatal deceits, not
" to be trufted. To perfons fuffering from
" eating any fpecies of fungi, the moft approv-
" ed and fpeedy remedy is to ufe emetics and
" cathartics," *Haller. Helvet. Hift.* p. 2338.

THE different vegetable poifons, of which we have hitherto treated, refemble each other very much in their effects. They all difturb the functions of the nervous fyftem, producing either vertigo, faintnefs, delirium, madnefs, ftupor, a paralytic ftate of the mufcles, or apoplectic fymptoms. Thefe appearances come on gradually; and if a vomit is given, or the ftomach fpontaneoufly rejects early the poifonous fubftance, health fpeedily returns. But if the poifon fhould have been taken in large quantities: if emetics cannot be conveyed into the ftomach, or the nerves fhould have been fo deadened as to be infenfible to their irritation, there is much reafon to fear that the cafe will terminate fatally.

WHEN any of the narcotic vegetable poifons have been unfortunately taken, the indications of cure will be,

1. To unload the ftomach by the fpeedy adminiftration of an active emetic.

2. To procure ftools either by proper cathartics, if the patient can fwallow them, or by the injection of irritating clyfters.

3. To

3. To correct and counteract the sedative effects of the poison, by giving from time to time draughts of some vegetable liquor, weak sparkling cyder or perry *. And,

4. IF any paralytic symptoms should remain, or the muscular action be much impaired, proper stimuli should be applied, such as synapisms and blisters; but more particularly the use of electricity is indicated.

BY observing these rules, I once saw a patient who had taken two ounces of the tinctura thebaica perfectly recover in two days.

THE poisons constituting the first class, in general have a virose disagreeable smell and taste: on the contrary, those which we are about to describe, appear by the evidence of the senses to be perfectly harmless. They speedily occasion epileptic symptoms. Of all epilepsies, these are the *most fatal;*——of all poisons, these are the most deadly. Pleasant

* Dr. Mead assures us, that he has given, with un-common success in these cases, a mixture of salt of wormwood and juice of lemons.—MEAD's WORKS, 4to edit. p. 128.

to the tafte, or inoffenfive to the palate, they pafs unfufpected into the ftomach; as foon as they take poffeffion there, they lock up both the doors; the upper and lower orifices are at the fame time fhut up by fpafms; nothing can be expelled, nor can any thing be got in: all poffibility of relief is cut off; and fhould that principle inherent in animal life, which tends to throw off every thing injurious to the machine, act, it produces thofe ineffectual heavings and ftruggles, which anfwer no other purpofes than to accelerate and increafe the effects of the poifon.

SOMETIMES, by fome fecret mode of operation, which we fhall probably never be acquainted with, they occafion *inftantaneous* death; and when this happens, no traces of the poifon can poffibly be difcovered; but if epileptic fymptoms take place, fuch appearances as epilepfy, either with or without poifon, neceffarily and fpecifically produces, may be expected.

AT a time when putrefaction is far advanced, and at a diftant period from death, fhould the face be difcovered of an intenfe

black

black colour, it may naturally be afked, from whence it arifes. Does putrefaction occafion it? if it does, why does not putrefaction *al-ways* give rife to this appearance? Why is not the body in general of the fame complexion? Is putrefaction, different in kind or degree, dependent on the different texture of the parts? certainly not: putrefaction is univer-fally the fame, and nature is always fimple and uniform in her operations. The black-nefs of the face is occafioned by putrefaction, but not by putrefaction only: if convulfions precede death, and the body becomes very putrid after it, the effect may be produced. I fhall attempt to explain it, by firft eftablifh-ing two facts (clear and demonftrable as the two firft propofitions of Euclid) upon which I mean to reafon.

THE firft propofition, then, which I fhall make, is this: As foon as an animal has breathed, and the foramen ovale is confe-quently fhut up, the blood muft pafs from the right fide of the heart, *through the lungs*, to the left fide of the heart, before it can cir-culate to any other part of the body.

F   THE

THE fecond is, That the human ſkin con-
ſiſts of three parts: the cutis, or true ſkin,
thick, porous, and vaſcular; the cuticle, or
ſcarf ſkin, thin, compact, and denſe; and
the rete mucoſum, a fine expanded mucous
membrane between them, more vaſcular in
the face than it is in any other part of the
body, and the ſeat of colour in men of all
complexions *.

IN an epileptic paroxyſm, reſpiration, which
depends upon muſcular action, is by ſpaſms
violently interrupted. Unleſs the lungs are
expanded, the blood cannot circulate through
the minute ramifications of the pulmonary
artery, from the right ſide of the heart to
the left. The vena cava, charged with all the
returning blood from the head, will be unable
to empty itſelf into the right auricle of the
heart, already full : hence, an accumulation

---

* In the blackeſt negroe which the coaſt of Africa
ever produced, the cutis is as white as the faireſt European, the colour reſides entirely in the rete mucoſum.
I viewed the human cuticle lately by a ſolar microſcope,
which magnified objects more than three million times,
and no perforations were to be ſeen ; ſo inconceivably
minute are thoſe pores which give paſſage to our in-
ſenſible perſpiration.

of

of blood will enfue in the head and face. The left ventricle of the heart, and the ofcillatory motion of the arteries, will exert a power to overcome the refiftance: but no more blood can be received by the vena cava, already overcharged. It muft therefore either be propelled into a feries of veffels, which in a ftate of health refufe admiffion to red blood, or the fmall arteries terminating in (what anatomifts call) red veins, will be ruptured, and their contents confequently thrown out into the cellular membrane under the fkin. When a mufcle is in action, it becomes pale; the fibres fwelling comprefs the interpofed veins, and forcibly expel their blood, while that of the arteries is denied an entrance: and if *all* the mufcles in a violent epilepfy are affected with convulfive fpafms, the greateft quantity of that blood which ufed to circulate through them, muft be deter- mined to other parts where there is lefs re- fiftance. The fluids, therefore, will either be propelled into the lymphatic fyftem, crowded into the veins, or extravafated in the cellular membrane. The equipoife of the circulation will be deftroyed; and the left ventricle of the heart, not receiving blood enough from

F 2

the

the lungs to excite irritation, contracts no more.;——it ceafes to beat.   At the time, or foon after death, the extravafated blood is not vifible through the fkin : but when the procefs of putrefaction takes place, an inteftine commotion enfues; an elaftic air, preffing *quaquaverfum*, diftends the body; the ftagnant blood is rendered both thinner and blacker; it foaks through the cutis, is refufed a paffage by the minute pores of the cuticle, and fpreading abroad, *dyes the rete mucofum of a black colour.*

C L A S S

CLASS II.

HEMLOCK DROPWORT.

OENANTHE foliis omnibus multifidis obtufis fubæqualibus. *Lin. Sp. Plant.* 365.

OENANTHE cicutæ facie Lobelii. *Park.* 894.

OENANTHE chærephylli foliis. *Bauh. Pin.* 162.

FILIPENDULA, cicutæ facie. *Gerard.* 1059.

OENANTHE, fucco virofo, cicutæ facie. *Lobel. J. B.*

OENANTHE maxima, fucco virofo, cicutæ facie. *Morif. Hift.*

OENANTHE tertia. *Matthioli*, p. 629.

THE root is long, thick, and tuberous, extremely fucculent, and on expofure to the external air, the juice becomes of a yellow complexion.

THE ftalk is ftriated, round, branched, and three feet high.

F 3 THE

THE leaves are of a pale green colour: they are large, fingly and doubly pinnated; each foliolum is wedge-fhaped, fmooth, ftriated with lines, and notched at the edges.

THE flowers are very fmall and white: they are difpofed in fmall umbels, placed upon the principal ftalks, with fhort ones at the fubdivifions. Each flower is compofed of five petals; fome of them are inflected and heart-fafhioned.

THE cup is large, and divided into five fegments.

THE feeds are ftriated on one fide, and dented on the other.

THIS plant is found upon the banks of the Thames, and many other rivers in England. It flowers in July.

HEMLOCK dropwort is one of the moft terrible poifons which the vegetable kingdom produces.

MR.

Mr. Lightfoot * fays, that he heard that celebrated botanic painter, the late Mr. Chriftopher Ehret, declare, that while he was drawing this plant, the fmell or effluvia only rendered him giddy, that he was feveral times obliged to quit the room, and walk out in the frefh air to recover himfelf: but recollecting at laft what might probably be the caufe of his repeated illnefs, he opened the doors and windows of his room, and the free air then enabled him to finifh his work without any more returns of giddinefs.

Eleven French prifoners had the liberty of walking in and about the town of Pembroke: three of them being in the fields a little before noon, found and dug up a large quantity of a plant with its roots, which they took to be wild celeri, to eat with their bread and butter for dinner. After wafhing it while in the fields, they all three eat, or rather tafted of the roots †.

As they were entering the town, without any previous notice of ficknefs at the ftomach,

* Flor. Scot. vol. i. p. 162.

† Letter from Mr. Howell, Surgeon at Haverfordweft, to Dr. Watfon. Phil. Tranf. N° 480, p. 229.

or

or diforder in the head, one of them was feized with convulfions. The other two ran home, and fent a furgeon to him. The furgeon endeavoured firft to bleed, and then to vomit him: but thofe endeavours were fruit-lefs, and the foldier died in a very fhort time.

IGNORANT yet of the caufe of their com-rade's death, and of their own danger, they gave of thefe roots to the other eight prifon-ers, who all eat fome of them with their dinner. The quantity could not be afcer-tained.

A FEW minutes after, the remaining two, who gathered the plants, were feized in the fame manner as the firft, of which one died; the other was bled, and a vomit with great difficulty forced down, on account of his jaws being, as it were, locked together. This operated, and he recovered, but he was for fome time affected with a giddinefs in his head: and it is remarkable that he was neither fick, or in the leaft difordered in his ftomach. The other eight, being bled and vomited *immediately*, were fecured from

the

the approach of any bad fymptoms. Upon examination of the plant, which the French prifoners miftook for wild celeri, Mr. Howell difcovered it to be the oenanthe aquatica cicutæ facie of Lobel, which grows very plentifully in the neighbourhood of Haver-fordweft. It is called by the common people there, five-fingered root, and is much ufed by them in cataplafms, for whitlows, &c. The perfons above referred to, eat only the root of the plant, without any of the ftalk or leaves.

* EIGHT young lads near Clonmel † in Ireland, miftook the roots of the oenanthe crocata, for the fium aquaticum, or water parfnep, and eat plentifully of them. A little time afterwards, going home, the eldeft, almoft an adult, without the leaft previous diforder or complaint, fell down backward, and died in convulfions. Four more died in the fame manner before the morning, not one of them having fpoken a fingle word from the moment the fymptoms firft appeared. Of the other three, one became furioufly

* Phil. Tranfact. Nº 238.
† In that part of Ireland, this plant is called Tahow.

mani-

maniacal, but recovered his senses the next day. The hair and nails of another fell off. Only one of the eight escaped without any harm, who ran home above two miles, and drank warm milk, which caused a diaphorefis.

A DUTCHMAN likewise was poisoned with the leaves of this plant, boiled in his pottage. He took the herb for smallage, to which its leaves have great resemblance *.

ALLEN † mentions an instance of four children who eat of the roots of the oenanthe cicutæ facie. They appeared all in great agonies, and afterwards were convulsed. Very fortunately, however, in their fits they vomited, which was encouraged by giving them large draughts of oil and warm water: and by great care and attention they all recovered.

STALPART Vander Wiel, in his Observations, takes notice of the fatal effects of

* Dr. Watson's account to the Royal Society. Phil. Tranf. N° 480. accompanied with an excellent plate of the plant.
                    † Synopf. Medicin.
                                        the

the roots of this plant, in two perfons who had miftaken them for thofe of the Macedonian parfley. Soon after eating the roots, they complained of violent heat in the throat and ftomach, attended with a vertigo, ficknefs at the ftomach, and purging. One of them bled at the nofe : the other was violently convulfed. Both died : one in two hours, the other in three. This cafe is accompanied with figures of the plant, but not very well executed.

THE fymptoms, which attended the above recited cafe, were different from thofe of the French prifoners at Pembroke : as in the latter there was no complaint of heat in the mouth or throat, nor did any ficknefs or diforder of the ftomach precede the convulfive paroxyfms.

THE oenanthe is very common in Cumberland, where the common people call it dead tongue, and apply it boiled in cataplafms to fome difeafes in their horfes *.

THE root of this plant has no ill tafte : hence it is the more dangerous to thofe whofe

* Threlkeld, Synopf. Plantar.

curiofity

curiofity or hunger may prompt them to eat it.

THE well-authenticated cafes we have produced, fufficiently demonftrate that, un-lefs timely prevented, epileptic fymptoms, convulfions, and death, will be the confe-quences of taking hemlock dropwort. If the root fhould have been fwallowed in a large quantity, or the violence of the fpafms prevent any thing being conveyed into the ftomach, no hope feems to remain : but if an active emetic can be given, either before the fymptoms come on, or foon after their appearance, the patient may probably recover. After he has vomited, he fhould drink, if poffible, large quantities of oil and water.

WATER

WATER HEMLOCK.

CICUTA umbellis oppofitifoliis, petiolis marginatis obtufis. *Lin. Sp. Pl.* 366.

CICUTA aquatica. *Gefner. Hort.* 254. *Wepfer. de Cicuta.*

CICUTA maxima quorundam. *Hort. Eyftet.*

SIUM majus anguftifolium. *Park.* 1241.

SIUM erucæ folio. *Bauh. Pin.* 154.

SIUM alterum olufatri facie. *Gerard.* 256. *Ray's Synopf.* 212.

SIUM alterum. *Dodon. Pempt.* 579.

SIUM foliis rugofis trifidis dentatis. *Morif. Umbel.* 63. tab. 5.

SIUM, pinnis laciniatis, pinnulis trifidis, nervo non foliofo. *Haller. Helv.* 436.

PHELLANDRIUM aquaticum. *Hill. Brit. Herb.* 412.

THE root is large and hollow, divided into cells by tranfverfe diaphragms; correfponding with which, the external furface

face is marked with circular depreſſions. At the beginning of winter, the root for the ſucceeding year is formed from the lower part of the ſtalk; and as the old root decays and rots, long white filaments are obſerved to extend themſelves from the new root, which ſhoot into the ſoil, and ſecure the ſituation of the plant. Before this proceſs takes place, the cells of the old root render it ſpecifically lighter than water: hence in winter, upon a ſudden riſe of the water, is is buoyed up to the ſurface, and frequently carried by the ſtream to a conſiderable diſtance from the place where it grew.

THE ſtalk is large, round, fiſtular, of a pale green colour, and divides near the top into numerous branches.

THE leaves are of a pale green: they are pinnated with ſingle, double, and triple foliola: each foliolum is ſpear-ſhaped, and finely ſerrated: the ſerratures are white at the tips.

THE flowers are ſmall and white: they ſtand upon large umbels at the tops of the branches.

branches. Each flower confifts of five petals, heart-fhaped and inflexed. The feeds are oval, and furrowed with three prominent meridians.

It flowers in June, and is common on the banks of feveral rivers in England : it is fond of the ftill, foft, muddy fides of lakes and ftagnant waters. *.

Although this plant is one of the moft deleterious which the vegetable kingdom produces, yet like the other poifonous plants before defcribed, it affords protection and nourifhment to various infects.

The chryfomela phellandria, and the gilt leptura, are found upon the roots, and the curculio paraplecticus within its ftems.

Dr. Withering † informs us, that early in the fpring when it grows in the water, cows often eat it, and are killed by it: but as the fummer advances, and its fmell be-

* Dr. Parfons met with it on the fide of Loch-End in Scotland. Lightfoot's Flor. Scot. vol. i. 165.

† Arrangement of Britifh Vegetables, vol. i. p. 176.

comes

comes ftronger, they carefully avoid it : hence the plant is fometimes called cow-bane. Although it is a certain and fatal poifon to cows, goats devour it greedily, and with impunity, and horfes and fheep eat it with fafety. Linnæus affures us, that he has known cattle die by eating the roots: and Wepfer fays that one ounce of it threw a dog into convulfions, and two killed him.

Schwenke, a German writer, gives an account of four boys who had the misfortune to eat of it, three of whom died in convulfions *.

In the month of March 1670, two boys and fix girls found the roots of the ciçuta aquatica in a meadow, and upon tafting them, perceiving they were not unpleafant, they all eat fome of them †.

The two boys, who eat a large quantity, were foon after feized with pains of the precordia, lofs of fpeech, an abolition of all the

* Schwenke, Catal. Stirp. & Foffil. Silefiæ.

† Wepfer, de Cicutæ Aquaticæ Hiftoria & Noxæ, p. 7.

fenfes,

fenfes, and terrible convulfions. The mouth was fo clofely fhut, that it could not be opened by any means. Blood was forced from the ears, and the eyes were horribly diftorted. Both the boys died in half an hour from the firft acceffion of the fymptoms. The fix girls, who had taken a fmaller quantity of the roots than the boys, were likewife feized with epileptic fymptoms, but in the intervals of the paroxyfms, fome Venus treacle diffolved in vinegar was given them; in confequence of which, they vomited and recovered : but one of them, the fifter of the boys who died, after fhe vomited, had a very narrow efcape for her life. She lay nine hours with her hands and feet out-ftretched and cold: all this time fhe had a cadaverous countenance, and her refpiration could fcarcely be perceived. When fhe recovered, fhe complained a long time of a pain in her ftomach, and was unable to eat any food, her tongue being much wounded by her teeth in the convulfive fits.

WEPFER has very minutely defcribed the fymptoms which took place in the firft boy, in the following words:

" JACOBUS

" Jacobus Mæder, puer sex annorum,
" domum rediit hilaris ac subridens, quasi re
" bene gesta : paulo post conquerebatur de
" præcordiorum dolore, & vix verbum effa-
" tus, humi prostatus urinam magno impetu
" ad viri altitudinem eminxit : mox terribili
" aspectu, cum omnium sensuum abolitione
" convulsus fuit, os arctissime clausit, ut
" nulla arte aperiri valuerit, dentibus stride-
" bat, oculos mire distorquebat, sanguis ex
" auribus promanabat ; circa præcordia tu-
" midam quoddam corpus pugni virilis mag-
" nitudine patris afflicti manum & miseran-
" di pueri præcordia, maxime circa cartila-
" ginem ensiformem, validissime feriebat :
" singultiebat crebro : vomiturus quandoque
" videbatur, nihil tamen ore arctissime clauso
" ejicere valuit : artus mire jactabat, & tor-
" quebat, sæpius caput retrorsum abripieba-
" tur, totumque dorsum incurvabatur in ar-
" cum : ut puellus subtus per spatium inter
" dorsum & stratum inoffense repere potu-
" isset.   Cessantibus convulsionibus per mo-
" mentum matris opem imploravit : mox
" pari ferocia illis redeuntibus nulla velli-
" catione, nulla acclamatione, nullove alio
" ingenio excitari poterat, donec viribus de-
                                " ficientibus

" ficientibus expalluit, & manu pectori ad-
" mota expiravit. Durarunt hæc fympto-
" mata vix ultra horam dimidiam. Poft
" obitum imprimis abdomen, & facies intu-
" muerunt abfque livore, nifi pauco circa
" oculos confpicuo. Ex ore cadaveris ufque
" ad horam fepulturæ fpuma viridis largiffime
" emanavit, & quamvis fæpius a patre mæftif-
" fimo deterfa fuiffet, mox tamen nova fuc-
" cedebat *."

* De Cicut. Aquat. p. 6.

LAUREL.

L A U R E L.

Lauro-cerafus. *Gerard. Cluf. J. Baub.*

Cerasus folio laurino. *C. Baub.*

Cerasus trapezuntina, five lauro-cerafus. *Park.*

THE root is large, tough, and furnifhed with many fibres.

The branches are woody, numerous,
brown on the outfide, and white within.

The leaves are large, flefhy, oblong,
fhining, pointed at both ends, and flightly
ferrated at the edges: their upper furface is
fmooth, and of a beautiful dark green colour;
the under fide is rough, ftrongly marked
with fibres, and of a light green complexion.

The flowers appear toward the fuperior
part of the branches: they are pentapetalous,

in

in five-leaved cups. They are followed by clufters of berries refembling cherries, and containing an oblong ftone within the pulp of the fruit. It flowers in May, and ripens its fruit in September.

The plant was firft brought from Trapezus, a city near the Euxine fea, to Cónftantinople, from thence into Italy, France, Germany, and England. This beautiful evergreen is now become very common in our gardens: it is eafily propagated, and bears very well the cold of northern climates.

The leaves of laurel have a bitter tafte, with a flavour refembling that of the kernels of the peach and apricot. They communicate an agreeable flavour to aqueous and fpirituous fluids, either by infufion or diftillation.

The diftilled water applied to the organs of fmelling ftrongly impreffes the mind with the fame ideas as arife from the *tafte* of bitter almonds, or apricot kernels: it is fo extremely deleterious in its nature, and fometimes fo fudden in its operation, as to occa-

G 3

fion

fion inftantaneous death *; but it more frequently happens that epileptic fymptoms are firft produced.

THIS poifon was difcovered by accident in Ireland in the year 1728. Before that time it was not an uncommon practice there to add a certain quantity of laurel water to brandy, or other fpirituous liquors, to render them agreeable to the palate. In the month of September 1728, at Dublin, three women drank fome laurel water, and one of them, Mary Whaley, a fhort time afterward, became violently difordered, loft her fpeech, and died in about an hour. Anne Boyce was feized in the fame manner, and died in a fhort fpace of time. Neither of them vomited. Frances Eaton, who drank no more than a fpoonful of the water, did not find herfelf indifpofed when the other

---

* A few fpoonfuls of laurel water killed a large dog whilft it was paffing down the throat, before it could be fuppofed to have reached the ftomach.——MEAD's WORKS, 4to. p. 128.

It was the cuftom of the late Dr. Nicholls, when he wanted dogs for anatomical purpofes, to give them ftrong laurel water, as the moft expeditious method of deftroying them.—BROMFIELD ON NIGHTSHADE, p. 75.

women

women were taken ill, but to prevent any bad confequence, took a vomit immediately, and no ill effects enfued *.

Dr. Madden faw Anne Boyce twenty-four hours after her deceafe, but he could not obtain leave from her friends to open the body. She was about fixty years of age, her countenance and fkin appeared of a natural colour, and her features were not altered. The abdomen was not fwelled, nor was there any other external mark of poifon.

Another accident of the fame kind happened in the town of Kilkenny: a young gentleman, fon to Mr. Evans of that place, miftook a bottle of laurel water for ptifan. It is uncertain what quantity he drank, but he died in a few minutes. This affair was not much regarded at that time, becaufe he laboured under a diftemper to which, or to an improper ufe of remedies, his death was attributed by thofe about him †.

* Phil. Tranf. N° 418. p. 84.

† Ibid. p. 48.

G 4 Dr.

Dr. Rutty of Dublin, in a letter to Dr.
Mortimer, dated May 17,. 1732, after obferving that fome people doubt.the poifonous
properties of laurel water,· thus proceeds:
" I can now confirm that it really is poifon-
" ous by the following inftance, the truth
" of which you may be affured of. . At Li-
" fininy, in Weftmeath, a girl of eighteen
" years of age, very well and healthy, took
" a quantity lefs than two fpoonfuls of the
" firft runnings of the fimple water of laurel
" leaves; whereupon within half a minute
" fhe fell down, was convulfed, foamed at
" the mouth, and died in a fhort time, .nor
" .was.there any fwellings in her body *."

Having procured fome laurel water, I
made with it the following experiments:

Experiment I,

March 17, 1781. In the prefence of
Dr. Simfon, two ounces of laurel water were
given to a large ftrong dog. Two minutes
after taking it, he appeared very uneafy, and
the mufcles of the back were affected with

* Phil. Tranfact. N° 452, p. 63.

fpafms,

fpafms. After making violent efforts to vomit, he brought up what we fuppofed the
greateft part of the water mixt with a thick
frothy mucus. In a little time he vomited
again, and in the fpace of three or four minutes by degrees recovered. One ounce more
of the water was then-given him, with which
he was fooner affected than with the firft
dofe: he breathed with difficulty, was fick,
and vomited fcon after; his head was drawn
backward by that kind of fpafm called opif-
thotonos. He fell down, and was fo generally convulfed that he feemed to be at the
point of death. The convulfions continued
fome minutes : he was placed upon his legs,
but they appeared paralytic, and he could
not ftand. In lefs than half an hour from
the time he took the firft dofe of laurel water, he perfectly recovered.

Experiment II.

March 20. One ounce of laurel water
was given to a young greyhound. Whilft
Dr. Rattray held the mouth open, I poured
the water into the dog's throat. As foon as
it was fwallowed, the doctor releafed his
head,

head, to obferve the effects of the poifon, when, to our great furprife, the dog fell down upon his fide, and without the leaft ftruggle, or any perceptible motion, was dead in a moment.

Experiment III.

March 22. One pint and a quarter of laurel water was given to a mare aged 28 years *. Within a minute from the time it was fwallowed, fhe feemed affected. Her flanks were obferved to heave much, and a trembling feized her limbs. In two minutes fhe fuddenly fell down upon her head, and a fhort time after was very violently convulfed. The convulfions continued about five minutes, at the expiration of which time, fhe lay ftill, but her breathing was very quick and laborious. Her eyes were much affected with continual fpafms: at this time four ounces more of the water were given her, after which fhe feemed much weaker, without any more convulfions,

* In prefence of Sir William Wheler, Dr. Rattray, and Mr. Snow, Surgeon.

and

and in about fifteen minutes from the time of her firft feizure, expired.

SOME little time before her death, a re-markable appearance was obferved in the carotid artery, through which the blood feemed to be very feebly pumped up in large globules, and not in a continued column, which feems to prove, that by the violence of the convulfions, the blood had been forced out of the arterial fyftem into the veins; and from the difficulty with which it circulated through the lungs, there was not a fufficient quantity tranfmitted into the left auricle of the heart to continue the circulation: hence death was the confe-quence.

DISSECTION.

UPON opening the abdomen, a ftrong fmell of laurel water was perceptible. The colon was not altered from its ufual appear-ance; but the fmall inteftines appeared of a purple colour, and their veins much diftended with blood. The ftomach contained fome hay, mixt with the laurel water. Its inter-nal

nal, furface was not inflamed, except, in a
fmall degree near the pyloris; and where a
number of botts were cluftered. The lungs
appeared remarkably full of blood; the
fmall veffels upon their furface being as rifi-
ble as if they had been injected with red
wax.

By experiments made on various animals
it appears, that the water of lauro-cerafus is
extremely dangerous; and whether we con-
fider the certainty of its effects, or the cele-
rity of its operation, it is as wonderful a
poifon as any we have heard of, not except-
ing that with which the Indians prepare their
arrows. Given by the mouth, or injected
into the rectum, its operation is equally
certain, and it acts the moment it touches
the ftomach, or is received into the inteftines.

THREE tea fpoonfuls of laurel water conveyed into the ftomach of an eel, killed it in
a few minutes; and it is well known that
eels will live fome time after their heads are
cut off. It is equally mortal to fmall animals, if applied to wounds of the mufcles,
and death is as certainly the confequence, as

if

if they had taken it into the ſtomach. A wound was made in the ſkin of the belly of a rabbit, about an inch in length, the muſcles were afterward ſlightly wounded in different places, and two or three tea ſpoonfuls of the water were applied to the part: in leſs than three minutes the animal fell down convulſed, and died ſoon after. This experiment was repeated, and the reſult was the ſame in different animals *.

THE water of lauro-ceraſus produces generally very ſtrong convulſions, and in a ſhort time death. The ſpaſmodic motions of the whole body are extremely violent, and the ſtruggles are fatal in a ſhort time.

Two tea ſpoonfuls only of the water were given to middle-ſized rabbits: they fell down convulſed in thirty ſeconds, and died within a minute.

WHEN it is given very ſtrong, and in large quantities to animals, they die almoſt inſtantly, and without convulſions, a ſudden

* Phil. Tranſact. vol. lxx. part 1. Append. xii.

and

and univerfal paralyfis coming on. If it is
taken in a fmaller quantity, the convulfions
are more or lefs ftrong : the hind feet firft lofe
their motion, and afterward the fore feet become paralytic. Upon diffection, no uncommon appearances are obfervable in the ftomach, nor any inflammation upon the inter-
nal membranes. The arterial fyftem is found
empty, and the veins very turgid with blood.
The finufes of the brain, and the veins of the
pia mater, have been feen very much diftended ; but thefe appearances may be better ex-
plained from the violence of the convulfions,
than from any fpecific properties of the
poifon.

In many refpects the poifon of lauro-cerafus, and the American poifon called ticunas,
agree in the fimilarity of their action *.
They both, when received into the ftomach,
occafion fudden agonies, and violent convulfive motions of the mufcles. Injected into
the rectum, the refult is the fame. When
they are applied to the large trunks of the
nerves, they produce no effects at all. If

* Abbè Fontana, on the American poifon call ticunas. Phil. Tranfact. vol. lxx. part 1.

they

they are brought into contact with wounds of the mufcles, death is the confequence. But they differ very effentially in this refpect. When the poifon called ticunas is injected into the large veins, it foon proves fatal; whereas the water of lauro-cerafus, mixt with the blood in the fame manner, produces no diforder, or any apparent effect.

THE Abbè Fontana having detached the fciatic nerve of a large rabbit more than an inch and a half, introduced under it a wrapper of very fine linen, fixteen times doubled, that the parts below it might not be penetrated by the water of the lauro-cerafus. He then wounded the nerve with many ftrokes of the lancet, in a longitudinal direction, and covered all this wounded part, which extended above eight lines in length, with a roll of cotton three lines in thicknefs, well fteeped in laurel water. More than fifteen drops were neceffary to moiften the cotton, and the fluid communicated itfelf directly by the wounds, to the medullary fubftance of the fciatic nerve. The whole was covered over about a minute after with new rags, fo that it was impoffible for the laurel water to touch

touch any other part but the wounded nerve. The external ſkin was ſewed up, and the animal was ſet at liberty: it ſeemed not to be in the leaſt affected either then or after-wards. It ran about, eat, and was as lively as ever. This experiment ſeems to prove, that the water of lauro-ceraſus applied immediately upon the nerves, and inſinuated into their medullary ſubſtance, is not at all poiſonous; conſequently that it does not act upon the nerves, however applied, externally.

The Abbè Fontana having obſerved, that the poiſon of the viper and the ticunas, like the lauro-ceraſus, were innocent applied to the nerves, but immediately killed ſtrong animals when introduced into the blood; it was extremely natural to conclude, that laurel water would have the ſame effects: experience, however, determines quite the contrary, and ſhews us that the mode of reaſoning by analogy, may ſometimes prove deceptive. He introduced ſome of the water into the jugular vein of a large rabbit, in the ſame manner as he had done the poiſon of the viper, and the American poiſon, yet the animal diſcovered no ſigns of ſuffering. He

ſuſpected

fufpected he had not performed the operation properly; that the fyringe might poffibly have infinuated itfelf into the cellular
membrane, and that he had not introduced
any of the water into the veffel : he therefore
repeated the experiment, and introduced into
the jugular vein a larger quantity of the poifon than he had hitherto employed, and was
careful to make the point of the fyringe enter
the veffel before he introduced the water;
yet ftill the animal was not affected by it,
but continued as lively as ever. He could
not perfuade himfelf to believe, that the
water of lauro-cerafus was not a powerful
poifon when introduced into the blood, fince
it was poifonous applied to wounds of the
mufcles, and when taken by the mouth, although it was harmlefs if brought into contact with the naked trunks of the nerves.
He therefore a third and a fourth time repeated the experiment, and introduced into
the blood a larger quantity of laurel water
than he had ufed before; but the refult was
in no refpect different from the former
effays *.

* Phil. Tranfact. vol. lxx.

H   Dr.

Dr. Mortimer gave to a puppy, one ounce and a half of laurel water: in two minutes time it became ſtrongly convulſed, put out the tongue, and made ſtrong efforts to vomit, but to no effect; it could not ſtand, but lay with its hinder legs ſtretched out: in five minutes it became more ſtrongly convulſed, rolled over and over ſeveral times, drew its head back to its rump, then lay on its ſide, and panted much : he ſtretched out his fore legs, one after the other, drawing in his flanks very quick: in fifteen minutes more he died. An hour after his death, Dr. Mortimer opened the body. All the contents of the abdomen were in their natural ſtate, the ſtomach was diſtended with wind, and contained a mucus of a much thicker conſiſtence than the liquor gaſtricus naturally is; the inſide of the ſtomach was *not at all inflamed.* Upon opening the thorax, he found the lungs a little redder than ordinary, with ſome veſſels on the outward membrane very turgid : upon taking them out of the cheſt, a large quantity of clear red blood iſſued from them. The veins and ventricles of the heart were turgid, and full of coagulated blood. There was no blood in the arteries:

the

the foramen ovale was open. The head was next examined: the dura mater appeared livid, as if bruifed; its veffels and the finus falciformis were turgid, and full of blood. The cortical fubftance of the brain looked of an unufual livid colour *..

THE doctor after this procured a middle-fized fpaniel, and poured fome laurel water down his throat: he ftruggled pretty much at firft, and whined, but when about an ounce and a half of it was down, he ceafed to ftruggle: an ounce more of the water was then given him: he was laid down on the ground, but never offered to get up, only ftretching out his legs, he expired directly. Soon after his death, Mr. Ranby opened him: the laurel water, with fome frothy mucus, was found in his ftomach: the veins in general were very turgid, but the blood was ftill fluid, and no alteration was found in any of the vifcera †.

DR. Porter forced three ounces of laurel water down the throat of a large dog: about

* Phil. Tranfact. Nº 420, p. 163.
† Ibid. N° 420.

two ounces of it were foon after difcharged by vomit : in a few minutes he became vio-lently convulfed, and in a fhort time after lay motionlefs, to all appearance was dying. Within ten minutes he vomited a fecond time, and threw up a fmall quantity of vifcid frothy matter, from which moment he began to recover, and within half an hour was per-fectly well *.

On the third of October, 1728, Dr. Madden gave a large fetting dog three ounces of laurel water. In three minutes he became ftrongly convulfed. The convulfions con-tinued five minutes : then a violent difficulty of breathing came on, which lafted about eight minutes, and gradually abated : upon which he endeavoured to raife himfelf, but could not. The doctor gave him an ounce and a half more, when he funk at once, and without any return of convulfions, or diffi-culty of breathing, he expired in two mi-nutes. Upon opening the ftomach, the doc-tor found therein the whole quantity of water he had taken : its furface was covered

* Phil. Tranfact. N° 420.

with

with froth, but it was not otherwise altered in its colour, confiſtence, or ſmell. The inſide of the ſtomach was *not in the leaſt inflamed*, nor was there any viſible alteration in the tunica villoſa. The veins of the ſtomach, all the meſaraic veins, and likewiſe the vena cava, were much diſtended with blood : the arteries, on the contrary, were remarkably empty. The liver and gallbladder were unaltered. The kidneys were unuſually full of blood, and appeared of a bluiſh colour, almoſt as deep as that of the violet plumb. Upon making an inciſion into one of the kidneys, the blood flowed in a much larger quantity than uſual. The heart exhibited no preternatural appearance *.

MANY ſimilar experiments were repeated by Dr. Madden, with nearly the ſame effects. He found that the ſymptoms were equally violent and fatal, if the laurel water was injected into the rectum. Violent convulſions were the uſual conſequence, and (what may appear ſurpriſing) that kind of ſpaſm called opiſthotonos was generally pro-

* Phil. Tranſact. N⁰ 418. p. 84.

duced.

duced. If the animal vomited, he either became better foon after, or recovered, unlefs more of the poifon was forced down the ftomach. The fpafms, however, which affected both orifices of the ftomach at the fame time, often prevented a rejection of the contents; and in that cafe there was no chance of recovery. In all the animals that were diffected, the *ftomach* and the abdominal vifcera were obferved free from *inflammation*, the arterial fyftem was *always* empty, and the veins remarkably diftended with fluid blood.

ALTHOUGH the poifon of laurel appears to confift in the effential oil brought over by diftillation, yet it is much to be fufpected that an infufion of its leaves may in fome cafes, and fome conftitutions, prove injurious. They have been in common ufe to give a flavour to cuftards, &c. but from an inftance I faw of their effects, this practice fhould not be continued.

JAN. 27, 1780, I was defired to vifit a young lady of an irritable habit of body. She was affected in the night with ficknefs: when

when I faw her fhe had cold fweats, an irregular pulfe, and fuch other fymptoms that
I fufpected fhe had taken fomething extremely noxious into her ftomach. Upon
enquiry, I was informed by her mother that
fhe had taken nothing which in her appre-
henfion could diforder her : that her fupper
the preceding evening had been very eafy of
digeftion, for that fhe had eaten nothing but
fome cuftard. Upon examination I found
the cuftards were very ftrongly flavoured
with laurel leaves. She continued ill a few
days, and afterward perfectly recovered.

F I N I S.

A N

E S S A Y

O N

ULINARY POISONS.

[Price ONE SHILLING.]

A N

E S S A Y

O N

CULINARY POISONS.

C O N T A I N I N G

C A U T I O N S

R E L A T I V E   T O   T H E

USE of LAUREL-LEAVES,

HEMLOCK, MUSHROOMS, COPPER-VESSELS,
EARTHEN JARS, &c.

W I T H

Obfervations on the ADULTERATION of BREAD
and FLOUR,

And the NATURE and PROPERTIES of WATER.

―――――――――――――

Unde fames homini vetitorum tanta ciborum ?
Audetis vefci, genus ô mortale ? quod, oro,
Ne facite ; et monitis animos advertite noftris.

OVID. MET. XV. 138.

―――――――――――――

L O N D O N.

Printed for G. KEARSLY, at No. 46, near Serjeants
Inn, Fleet-Street.

M,DCC,LXXXI.

CONTENTS.

page

Of the Lauro-Cerafus, or common
   Laurel,   -   -   9
Hemlock   -   -   12
Mufhrooms   -   -   13
Copper veffels   -   -   15
The folution or falt of lead   -   21
Brown earthen ware, &c.   -   ib.
Of the adulteration of bread and flour   25
Of WATER.   -   -   28
Rain water   -   -   31
Snow water   -   -   33
Spring water   -   -   35
Stagnant water   -   -   36
Pump water   -   -   ib.
Thames and New-River water   39
Methods, by which water may be ob-
   tained in its greateft purity   -   40

P R E-

PREFACE.

MANKIND are fubject to innumerable difeafes, from which other animals are exempted. But from whence do thefe difeafes arife? From the feeds of mortality in the human frame? From luxury and intemperance? Or from an indifcreet ufe of vegetable and mineral poifons in the preparation of our food? ---From the laft of thefe fources we certainly derive many troublefome, and fometimes fatal diforders : fo that, on many occafions, we may exclaim with the fons of the prophets*, " There is death in the pot!"

* 2 Kings iv. 40.

The

The defign of this publication is to guard people againſt theſe diſaſters; and, if poſſible, to prevent ſome of the calamities of human life. If it ſhould anſwer this uſeful purpoſe, the author's ambition will be fully gratified.

ON

CULINARY POISONS.

1. The LAURO-CERASUS, or Common LAUREL.

THE water diftilled from the leaves of this tree has been frequently mixed with brandy, and other fpirituous liquors, in order to give them the flavour of ratifia; and the leaves are often ufed in cookery, to communicate the fame kind of tafte to cream, cuftards, puddings, and fome forts of fweetmeats: But, in the year 1728, an account of two women dying fuddenly in Dublin, after drinking fome of the common diftilled laurel water, gave rife to feveral experiments, made upon dogs, with the diftilled water, and with the infufion of the leaves of the

B   lauro-

lauro-cerafus, communicated by Dr. Madden, phyfician at Dublin, to the Royal Society in England, and afterwards repeated (in the year 1731) and confirmed by Dr. Mortimer, F. R. S. by which it appeared, that both the water and the infufion brought on convulfions, palfy, and death, when taken by the mouth, or anus *.

Dr. Mead † fpeaks of the foregoing accident and experiments in thefe terms : " A fmall quantity of this water killed two women, who drank it, very fuddenly. Hereupon a learned phyfician, furprized at the event, (this plant having never been thought to be any wife noxious) made feveral experiments with it upon dogs, which were afterwards, fome of them, repeated here, with the fame fatal fuccefs."

Dr. Mortimer affirms, " that laurel-water is equally mortal with the bite of the rattle-fnake, and more quick in its operations than any mineral poifon."

* See Philofophical Tranfaftions, No. 418, and 420.

† Mead on Poifons, Effay v.

Dr.

Dr. James fays : "laurel-water is the moft de-leterious poifon perhaps known, killing almoft inftantaneoufly ‡."

The laurus of the ancients, or the *bay*, is, on the contrary, of a falutary nature, and of ufe in fe-veral diforders.

It may be faid, that the laurel in cuftards, and other articles of cookery, is ufed in very fmall quantities, and has never been attended with any pernicious effect.——But, I afk, who can pretend to affert, that it has not occafioned fome latent diforder, or fome complaints, which have been afcribed to other caufes? What perfon of fenfe or prudence would truft to the difcretion of an ig-norant cook, in the ufe of a dangerous ingredient in his puddings or cuftards? Or, who, but a madman, would choofe to feafon his victuals with poifon?

The remedy is from ten to forty drops of fal ammoniac, in a glafs of water, repeated as the fymptoms may require.

‡ James's Difpenfatory, book iii. c. 1. p. 228.

2. Small

2. Small HEMLOCK, or FOOLS PARSLEY.

DESCRIPTION.

The firſt leaves are divided into numerous ſmall parts, which are of a pale green, oval, pointed, and deeply indented. The ſtalk is ſlender, round, upright, ſtriated, and about a yard high. The flowers are white, growing at the tops of the branches in little umbells. It is an annual plant, common in orchards and kitchen gardens, and flowers in June and July. This plant has been often miſtaken for parſley: and from thence it has received the name of *Fools Parſley.*

Though it ſeems not to be of ſo virulent a na-ture as the larger hemlock, yet Boerhaave places it among the vegetable poiſons, in his Inſtitutes; and, in his Hiſtory of Plants, produces an in-ſtance of its pernicious effects ‡. It is therefore

‡ Inſtitutes, § 1138, Hiſt. of Plants, p. 93.

fore neceffary to guard againſt it in collecting herbs for ſallads, and other purpoſes.

---

3. MUSHROOMS.

Muſhrooms have been long uſed in ſauces, in ketchup, and other forms of cookery. They were highly eſteemed by the Romans, as they are at preſent, by the French, Italians, and other nations.

Pliny exclaims againſt the luxury of his countrymen in this article; and wonders, what extraordinary pleaſure there can be, in eating ſuch *dangerous fcod**. The ancient writers on the Materia Medica ſeem to agree, that muſhrooms are in general unwholeſome; and ·the moderns, Lemery, Allen, Geoffroy, Boerhaave, Linnæus, and others, concur in the ſame opinion. There are numerous inſtances upon record of their fatal effects. Al-

---

* Quæ voluptas tanta *ancipitis* cibi? Plin. Nat. Hiſt, xxii. 23.

Almoſt all of them, as the laſt-mentioned author affirms, " are fraught with poiſon †."

The common eſculent kinds, if eaten too freely, frequently bring on heart-burns, ſickneſſes, vomitings, diarrhœas, dyſenteries, and other dangerous ſymptoms. It is therefore to be wiſhed, that they were baniſhed from the table. But, if the palate muſt be indulged in theſe treacherous gratifications, or, as Seneca ‡ calls them, this " voluptuous poiſon", it is neceſſary, that they, who are employed in collecting them, ſhould be extremely cautious, left they ſhould collect ſuch as are abſolutely pernicious ; which, conſidering to whoſe care this is generally committed, may, and undoubtedly has, frequently happened §.

† Fungi plerique VENENO TURGENT. Linnæi Amæn· Acad. vol. I.

‡ Quid tu illos boletos, VOLUPTARIUM VENENUM, nihil occulti operis judicas facere, etiamſi præſentanei non furant? SEN. EP. 95.

§ See Gentleman's Magazine, December, 1755 ; and Supplement, September, 1757.

The

The eatable mufhrooms at firft appear of a roundifh form, like a button ; the upper part and the ftalk are very white ; the under part is of a livid flefh-colour ; but the flefhy part, when broken, is very white. When thefe are fuffered to remain undifturbed, they will grow to a large fize, and expand themfelves almoft to a flatnefs, and the red part underneath will change to a dark colour.

COPPER VESSELS.

Copper, when it is handled, yields an offenfive fmell, and if touched with the tongue, a fharp pungent tafte, and even excites a naufea. Verdegris is nothing but a folution of this metal by vegetable acids. And it is well known, that a very fmall quantity of this folution will produce cholics, vomitings, intolerable thirft, univerfal

con-

convulfions, and other dangerous fymptoms. If thefe effects, and the prodigious divifibility of this metal be confidered, there can be no doubt of its being a violent and fubtile poifon. We are daily expofed to this poifon by the prefent ufe of copper veffels for dreffing our food. The very air of the kitchen, abounding with oleaginous and faline particles, penetrates and difpofes them to diffolution, before they are ufed. Water, by ftanding fome time in a copper veffel, is impreg-nated with verdegris, as may be demonftrated by throwing into it a fmall quantity of any volatile alkali, which will immediately tinge it with a paler or deeper blue, in proportion to the ruft contained in the water. Vinegar, apple-fauce, greens, oil, greafe, butter, and almoft every other kind of food, will extract the verdegris in a greater degree. It is true, people imagine, that the ill effects of copper are prevented by its being tinned : but the tin, which adheres to the copper, is fo extremely thin, that it is foon penetrated by the verdegris, which infinuates itfelf through the pores of that metal, and appears green upon the furface.

M. Amy,

M. Amy, of the Academy of Sciences at Paris, obferves, that "verdegris is one of the moft vio- lent poifons in nature:" yet, fays he, " rather than quit an old cuftom, the greater part of man- kind are content to fwallow fome of this poifon every day". Amy's Treat. upon Cifterns, printed at Paris, 1750.

M. Thiery, in a thefis, which is added to this tract, has more particularly confidered the nox- ious qualities of copper, and the various means, by which they may be communicated to what- ever we eat or drink. " Our food, fays he, re- ceives its quantity of poifon in the kitchen, by the ufe of copper pans and difhes. The brewer mingles poifon in our beer, by boiling it in a copper. Salt is diftributed to the people from copper fcales, covered with verdegris." Pickled cucumbers are rendered green by an infufion of copper coin. " The paftry-cook bakes our tarts in copper patty-pans. But confections and fyrups have greater powers of deftruction : for they are fet over a fire in copper veffels, which have not been tinned; and the verdegris is plen- tifully extracted by the acidity of the compofi- tion. And though we do not, after all, fwallow

C   death

death in a single dose, yet it is certain, that a
quantity of poison, however small, which is repeated with every meal, must produce more fatal
effects, than is generally believed".

Bell-metal kettles are very often used in boiling
cucumbers for pickling, in order to make them
green. This is an absurd and dangerous practice,
If the cucumbers acquire any additional green-
ness by the use of these kettles, they can only derive it from the copper, of which they are made.

According to some writers, bell-metal is a
composition of tin and copper, or pewter and
copper, in the proportion of twenty pounds of
pewter, or twenty-three pounds of tin, to one
hundred weight of copper. According to others,
this metal is made of copper, a thousand pounds;
tin, from two to three hundred pounds; and brass,
one hundred and fifty pounds *.

Spoons and other kitchen utensils are frequently made of a mixed metal, called alchemy; or,
as it is vulgarly pronounced, ockimy. The rust
of this metal, as well as the former, is highly pernicious.

* Lord Bacon's Phys. Remains.

White

White alchemy is made of pan-brafs, one pound; and arfenicum, three ounces. Red alchemy is made of copper, and auripigmentum, or orpiment †.

The author of a tract, entitled, Serious Reflections on the dangers attending the ufe of copper veffels, publifhed at London in 1755, afferts, that " the greater frequency of palfies, apoplexies, madnefs, and all the frightful train of nervous diforders, which fuddenly attack us, without our being able to account for the caufe, or which gradually weaken our vital faculties, are the poifonous effects of this pernicious matter, taken into the body infenfibly with our victuals, and thereby intermixed with our blood and juices".

However this may be, it is certain, that there have been innumerable inftances of the pernicious confequences of eating food dreffed in copper veffels, not fufficiently cleaned from this ruft. On this account the Senate of Sweden, about the year 1753, prohibited copper veffels, and ordered, that none, but fuch as were made of iron, fhould be ufed in their fleets and armies.

† Lord Bacon's Phyf. Remains.

But

But if copper veffels are ftill continued, every
cook and good houfewife fhould be particularly
careful in keeping them clean and well tinned;
and fhould fuffer, nothing to remain in them longer, than it is abfolutely neceffary for the purpofe
of cookery.

REMEDY.

" The common cure, fays Dr. Mead, of all
poifons taken into the ftomach, muft be by
throwing them up again, by vomiting, as foon as
poffible, and defending the membranes from their
pungent acrimony. Drinking very large quantities of warm milk, with oil of fweet almonds,
till the vomiting ceafes, will anfwer the firft in-
tention. The other, in mineral poifons, (for the
effects of vegetable poifons, after they have been
vomited up, generally go off by diluting plentifully with foft and fat liquids) requires particular
care, which may be in this way. The force of
thefe depends upon a combination of metallic
particles with faline cryftals: therefore the dif-
uniting of thefe muft deftroy their power. This
may

may be done by drinking a quantity of a lixivium made by a folution of falt of tartar in water : for this falt, uniting with the corrofive cryftalline falt, will, after fome degree of effervefcence, kill it, as the chemifts fpeak ; by which means, being difengaged from the mineral globules, it will be rendered of no effect"*.

The SOLUTION or SALT of LEAD.

Lead is a metal eafily corroded, efpecially by the warm fteams of acids, fuch as vinegar, cyder, lemon-juice, rhenifh wine, &c. And this folution, or falt of lead, is a flow and infidious, though certain poifon. The glazing of all our common brown pottery ware, is either lead or lead ore. If black, it is lead ore, with a fmall proportion of manganefe, which is a fpecies of iron ore. If yellow, the glazing is lead ore, and appears yellowifh by having fome pipe or white clay

* Mead on Poifons, Effay iv.

clay under it. The colour of the common pottery ware is red, as the veffels are made of the
fame clay with common bricks. Thefe veffels
are, fo porous, that they are penetrated by all
falts, acid or alkaline, and are unfit for retaining
any faline fubftance. They are improper, though
too often ufed, for preferving four fruits or
pickles. The glazing of fuch veffels is corroded
by the vinegar; for, upon evaporating the liquor,
a quantity of the falt of lead will be found at the
bottom. A fure way of judging, whether the vinegar, or other acids, have diffolved part of the
glazing, is, by their becoming vapid, or lofing
their fharpnefs, and acquiring a fweetifh tafte by
ftanding in them for fome time : in which cafe
the contents are to be thrown away as pernicious.

The fubftance of the pottery ware commonly
called Delft, the beft being made at Delft in
Holland, is a whitifh clay when baked, and foft,
as not having endured a great heat in baking.
The glazing is a compofition of calcined lead,
calcined tin, fand, fome coarfe alkaline falt, and
fandiver; which being run into a white glafs, the
white colour being owing to the tin, is afterwards
ground

ground in a mill, then mixed with water, and the veffels, after being baked in the furnace, are dipped into it, and put into the furnace a fecond time ; by which means, with a fmall degree of heat, the white glafs runs upon the veffels. This glazing is exceedingly foft and eafily cracks. What effects acids will have upon it, the author of thefe obfervations cannot fay, not having tried them : but they feem to be improper for infpiffating the juice of lemons, oranges, or any other acid fruits.

The moft proper veffels for thefe purpofes are porcelain or china ware. The fubftance of them is of fo clofe a texture, that no faline, or other liquor, can penetrate them. The glazing, which is made likewife of the fubftance of the china, is fo firm and clofe, that no falt or faline fubftance can have the leaft effect upon it. It muft, however, be obferved, that this remark is only applicable to the porcelain made in China : for fome fpecies of the European manufactory are certainly glazed with a fine glafs of lead, &c.

Next to china is the ftone ware, commonly called the Staffordfhire ware. The fubftance of
thefe

thefe veffels is a compofition of black flint, and a ftrong clay, that bakes white. Their outfides are glazed by throwing into the furnace, when well heated, common or fea falt decrepitated ; the fteam or acid of which, flying up among the veffels, vitrifies the outfides of them, and gives them the glazing. This ftone ware does not appear to be injured or affected by any kind of falts, either acid or alkaline, or any liquors, hot or cold. They are therefore extremely proper for all common ufes, but require a careful management, as they are much apter to crack with any fudden heat, than china.

The Heffian ware, or the veffels made of the fame fubftance with the Duke d'Alva's bottles, commonly called grey-beards, feem to be made of ftrong pipe clay, mixed with fand, and glazed in the baking, by the alkaline falt, which arifes from the wood uied in baking them, wood having always the effect, when the furnace is intenfe, to vitrify the outfide of all clays*.

* Differt. by James Lind, M. D.

REMARKS

REMARKS on the ADULTERATION of BREAD and FLOUR.

Extracted from a Treatife " On the nature of bread, honeftly and difhoneftly made", publifhed in 1757, by JAMES MANNING, M. D.

The author tells us, that in the fophiftication of flour, mealmen and bakers have been known to ufe bean meal, chalk, whiting, flaked lime, alum, and even afhes of bones. The firft, bean flour, is perfectly innocent, and affords a nourifhment equal to that of wheat; but there is a toughnefs in bean flour, and its colour is dufky. To remove thefe defects, chalk is added to whiten it, alum to give the whole compound that confiftence, which is neceffary to make it knead well in the dough, and jalap to take off the aftringency. It may be fuppofed, that thefe horrid iniquities are only imaginary, or at leaft exaggerated, and that fuch mixtures muft

D   be

be difcoverable even by the moft ordinary tafte; but as fome adulterations of this nature have certainly been practiced, the following experiments may ferve to gratify curiofity, or difcover frauds, where any fuch exift.

" To difcover whether flour be adulterated with whiting or chalk, mix with it fome juice of lemon or good vinegar. If the flour be pure, they will remain together at reft ; but if there be a mixture of whiting or chalk, a fermentation, like the working of yeft, will enfue. The adulterated meal is whiter and heavier than the good : the quantity that an ordinary tea-difh will contain, has been found to weigh more than the fame quantity of genuine flour, by four drachms, and 19 grains, Troy.

" The regular method to detect thefe frauds in bread is this : cut the crum of a loaf into very thin flices ; break them, but not into very fmall pieces, and put them into a glafs cucurbit, with a large quantity of water. Set this, without fhaking, in a fand furnace, and let it ftand, with a moderate warmth, four and twenty hours. The crumb of the bread will in this time foften in all
its

its parts, and the ingredients will feperate from it. The alum will diffolve in the water, and may be extracted from it in the ufual way. The jalap, if any have been ufed, will fwim upon the top in a coarfe film, and the other ingredients, being heavy, will fink to the bottom. This is the beft and moft regular method of finding the deceit; but as cucurbits, and fand furnaces, are not at hand in private families, there is a more familiar method.

" Let the crum of a loaf be fliced as before directed, and put it, with a great deal of water, into a large earthen pipkin. Let this be fet over a very gentle fire, and kept a long time mode- rately hot; and the pap being poured off, the bone afhes, or other ingredients, will be found at the bottom."

ON

On WATER.

Obſervations on Water, extraćted from Dr.
Rotherham's Philoſophical Enquiry, &c.

IT is a long eſtabliſhed obſervation, that the
beſt waters boil and cool again the ſooneſt ;
and that they evaporate in the leaſt time, and with
the leaſt degree of heat.

A well known mark of the purity of water is its
ſoftneſs. This quality is diſcoverable by the
touch, if we only waſh our hands in it: and the
diſtinćtion between hard and ſoft water generally
ariſes from its difficult or eaſy union with oily
ſubſtances.

Soft

Soft water is the moft proper for the wafhing and bleaching of linen, the making of paper, and for moft medicinal purpofes. It mixes more uniformly with milk, and does not curdle it, as hard waters frequently do. It boils peafe and beans fofter, and mixes better with flour, rice, oatmeal, &c. In boiling meat it gives it a more agreeable colour than hard water, which often boils it red.

There are however fome purpofes, to which hard water is more proper : as, in feveral kinds of dying; in making ftarch; and in the rincing of foap out of linen, after it has been wafhed ; as it is obferved to give the linen a better colour, and an agreeable firmnefs or crifpnefs; but the linen thus treated requires more foap, when it comes to be wafhed again. Hard water gives a better colour to greens, and a firmnefs to all forts of fifh, efpecially cod, when boiled in it.

The Burton, Nottinghamfhire, Liverpool, and feveral other kinds of ale, which are much admired, are faid to be brewed with hard water. But Dr. Mead and others condemn the ufe of thefe liquors, as productive of various diforders, and particularly the cholic.

From

From thefe remarks we may reafonably infer, that hard water cannot fo well anfwer the purpofes of diluting and digefting our food ; as it will not fo readily mix and unite with the different parts of it, nor affimulate and digeft them properly. Befides the large quantities of acid and nitrous falts, with the loads of felenite and calcareous earth, which thefe waters generally contain, will naturally difpofe them to form obftructions, when, by the courfe of circulation, thefe folid particles come into the minuteft veffels, more efpecially thofe of the glands. Hence they are often blamed, as laying the foundation of fcrophulous, ftrumous, and other glandular fwellings and obftructions.

It is from the quantity of ftony matter, which the hard waters generally contain, that moft of them have large incruftations upon the fides of the veffels, in which they are boiled; and they have by fome been difapproved for this reafon, as caufing the ftone. But the calculous concretions in the bladder and kidneys are of a very different nature from thefe incruftations ; and, as Dr. Heberden juftly obferves, " they totally differ from all foffil ftones in every thing except the name; and the

pre-

pretended experience of the effects of certain stony waters in breeding the stone, may, upon the best authorities, be rejected as false*.

The best way of determing the hardnefs or softnefs of water, is by scraping any certain quantity of soap into it, and obferving how it dissolves or lathers. If water be perfectly soft, the soap will dissolve quickly, uniformly, and without curdling ; and, upon shaking the glafs briskly, will raife a strong froth or lather at the top. But the smalleft degree of hardnefs will shew itself, either by the soap not dissolving so readily, by its turning curdly and uneven, or by less froth remaining after it is agitated ; and the different degrees of hardnefs may hereby be very well determined. The best way of making this trial is with a small quantity of Castile soap, viz. about a grain to an ounce of water.

RAIN - WATER.

In summer-time rain-water brings along with it the feeds and embryos of vegetables and animalcula,

† Medical Tranf. by the Coll. of Phyf. vol. 1. p. 7.

malcua, which render it difagreeable to the tafte, and promote its putrefaction. If it be kept in wooden veffels, it will foon ftink, and become unfit for ufe; and then, if it be viewed with a microfcope, it will be found to contain an amazing number of various animalcula; and particularly thofe, which, from their form and motion, are called the wheel animals*. Thefe animalcula are fuppofed to be the chief caufe of the water's putrefaction.

Rain water is a little hard, when it firft falls; but in two or three days it becomes perfectly foft.

The rain, which falls through the fmoke of large towns, is rendered foul and black; more especially if it be collected, as it generally is, from the roofs of houfes; when it brings with it a great many particles of foot, which give it a very difagreeable tafte and colour. Where the tiles are blackened by the fmoke of glafs-houfes, &c. the water,

---

* Baker's Mifcrofcope made eafy, p. 83. Employment for theMicrofcope, p. 295.

water, which falls from them, is unfit for almoſt any domeſtic purpoſes.

When rain-water ſubſides, and is well filtered, it becomes perfectly clear and bright. If it be kept in wooden veſſels, it contracts a particular ſmell, taſte and colour from the wood.

Clean earthen jars are the beſt for keeping water. Though leaden ciſterns may be uſed with ſafety, if they be kept clear from vegetable acids; all of which are found to corrode lead, and to produce a very noxious ſalt. The veſſels, in which water is preſerved, ſhould be covered, to prevent any duſt or filth from getting in; and the water will be more agreeable, if kept in a cool place.

SNOW-WATER.

Some of the greateſt philoſophers and phyſicians have differed much in their opinion of ſnow-water. Hippocrates, Hoffman, and others, condemn it: But Boerhaave, on the other hand, is

E   la-

lavifh in its encomiums. He afferts, that fnow, which is collected from the tops of high fandy mountains, at a diftance from any towns or houfes, where it has fallen after a long fharp froft, in calm weather, and lies at a confiderable height above the furface of the earth, produces water, " which is the pureft of all, quite immutable, capable of being kept for many years, and is a fingular re-medy for inflammations of the eyes" *.

Dr. Rotheram having mentioned the efficacy of fnow-water in burns, and in fertilizing the ground, relates the following experiment, which, though it may appear of a trivial nature, he very juftly remarks, is not below the notice of a philo-fopher.

" One effect of fnow, of which I do not remember any where to have read, is, that a certain quantity of it, taken up frefh from the ground, and mixed in a flour-pudding, will fupply the place of eggs, and make it equally light. The quantity al-lotted is two table fpoonfuls, inftead of one egg ; and if this proportion be much exceeded, the pud-ding will not adhere together, but will fall to pieces in boiling. I affert this from the expe-rience

* Boerh. Chem. vol. 1. p. 349. London edit. 1735.

rience of my own family; and any one, who choofes to try it, will find it to be a fact".

SPRING WATER.

As all our fprings are originally fupplied by rain, or melted fnow, and hail, ftrained through the pores and cavities of the earth, their waters will vary according to the different foils, or ftrata, through which they pafs. If waters meet with nothing in their fubterraneous paffages, which will unite with them, or diffolve in them, they iffue out in their greateft purity. The fprings, which come from gravel, fand, or fome light and porous ftones, are generally the pureft, and beft; for the water being filtered through their fmall pores, is cleared from almoft every foreign fubftance or impurity, which it had contracted in the air; acquires an agreeable coolnefs, and becomes limpid, bright, and fparkling.

But, as there are few foils, which do not contain fome kinds of falt, or other mineral fubftances, which are foluble in water, moft of our fprings are found to partake, in fome meafure, of

E 2   the

the nature of the foil, through which they pafs, and are innocent, falutary, or noxious, in proportion to the quantity, kind, or mixture, of the various ingredients, of which they are compofed; and the conftitution, of the perfon, who ufes them : and fome of them are of great medicinal efficacy.

STAGNANT WATER.

Stagnant water in ponds and ditches is generally efteemed the worft. But large lakes, which are kept in almoft a continual agitation by the wind, do not properly come within the denomination of ftagnant waters.

PUMP WATER, efpecially in LONDON.

It appears from the analyfis performed by Dr. Heberden †, that feveral pump waters in London, which he had examined, and probably moft

of

† See Medical Tranfact. vol. 1.

of them, contain powder of lime-ftone, and the mineral acids of vitriol, nitre, and fea-falt, united in various proportions. Thefe waters are likewife tainted with an oilinefs, which gives them a remarkably yellcwifh caft, when compared with pure diftilled water. It is reafonable to think, that waters impregnated with fuch active fubftances, in a quantity fufficient to render them difagreeable to the tafte, cannot always be drunk with impunity. They have accordingly been fufpected of occafioning pains in the ftomach and bowels, glandular tumors and coftivenefs, where the fimple lime-ftone prevails ; and diarrhœas, where much of it is united with the folution of a-cids; and it is probable, that a continued ufe of fuch water may be the caufe of many other diforders, efpecially to the infirm, and to children. From whence it follows, that a change of place may often be of as much ufe to weak perfons, from the change of water, as of air.

Some obfcure notion of the unwholefomenefs of pump water, induces many perfons to boil it, and let it ftand to grow cold ; by which it will indeed be made to part from moft of its un-neutralized lime-ftone and felenite ; but at the fame time it will become more ftrongly impreg-
nated

nated with the faline matter, and therefore it will
be worfe.

If a fmall quantity of falt of tartar were added
to the water, it would readily precipitate both the
loofe lime-ftone, and likewife that which is united
to the acids. Ten or fifteen grains would generally be enough for a pint; but the exact proportion would readily be found, by continuing to
add to it, by little and little, till it ceafed to occafion white clouds. This is an eafy way, not
only of freeing the water from its lime-ftone, but
alfo of changing the faline part into nitre and fal
fylvii, both of which we know, by long experience, to be innocent.

But the beft way of avoiding the bad effects of
pump water would be, not to make a conftant
ufe of it; and in a place fo well fupplied with
river water as London, there is very little necef-
fity to drink of the fprings, which in fo large a
city, befides their natural contents, muft collect
many additional impurities from cellars, burying-
grounds, common-fewers, and many other offenfive places, with which they undoubtedly often
com-

communicate ; fo that it is indeed a wonder, that
we find this water at all tolerable *.

T H A M E S and N E W - R I V E R
W A T E R.

River waters partake of the properties of their
fprings, and the channels, through which they
run ; yet, in a wonderful manner, they foon free
themfelves from their impurities. The motion of
the current †, the abforption of the foil, the fun
and rain, have each of them a confiderable fhare
in this effect.

The Thames water, efpecially in the neighbourhood of London, is mixed with many impure
ingredients. It is faid to become offenfive in feven or eight days, or fometimes fooner, if it be
kept in unfeafoned cafks. In this ftate it gene-
rates a quantity of foul inflammable air, as may
be feen by holding the flame of a candle to the
bung-hole of a cafk when it is firft opened. But
by

* See Medical Tranfact. vol. 1.

† The moft rapid rivers contain, cæteris paribus, the
pureft water.

by this fermentation it foon purifies itfelf; and by opening the bung, it will often become fweet in twenty-four hours, and fooner, if it be poured from one veffel to another, or ventilated *.

METHODS, BY WHICH WATER MAY BE OBTAINED IN ITS GREATEST PURITY.

As it appears, that almoft all the water ufed in cookery is tainted with impure ingredients ; rain water, with a great variety of volatile bodies, fuligi-nous particles, exhalations, invifible feeds, and in-fects; river, pond, and well water, with a mixture of foil and mud, decayed vegetables, and the fpawn of vermin, it will be very proper to purify it, before it is ufed for drinking, or any culinary purpofe. This may be done by various contrivances.

1. The water of the Thames, and that of the New River, are very often muddy, or tafte ftrongly of weeds and leaves. Dr. Heberden ac-knowledges, that the latter fault cannot eafily be

re-

* Philof. Tranf. No. 127, 268. Boerh. Elem. of Chem. vol. 1. p. 333. Rotheram's Philof. Inquiry.

remedied ; but, he obferves, they would foon be freed from their muddinefs, if kept fome time in an open jar : and he is of opinion, that if the water given to very young children, were thus purified, it might prevent fome of their bowel-diforders, and fo contribute a little to leffen that amazing mortality among the children, which are nurfed in London.

2. Rain water, when grown putrid, as Boerhaave affures us, may be eafily rendered wholefome again, and may be drunk without being offenfive, by only boiling it a few moments : for by this expedient, the animals that are in it will be deftroyed, and, with the reft of the impurities, will fubfide to the bottom. If then, fays he, you make it moderately acid, by adding to it a fmall quantity of acid that is very ftrong, it will be fit for ufe. This is found to be of excellent fervice under the Equator, and between the Tropics, where the waters putrify in a horrible manner, and breed a multitude of infects, and yet muft be drunk. For the fame reafon, a fmall quantity of fpirit of vitriol, mixed with water, will prevent its growing putrid, and breeding any animals, and,

F

at the fame time, preferve it wholefome and good *.

3. A common way of purifying water is by filtration. Water, which is filterated through porous ftones, is extremely clear and limpid; but fome writers have afferted, that it acquires a petrifying quality in its paffage, which, at length, may produce difagreeable effects ‡. However this may be, thefe ftones are too dear for common ufe.

Dr. Rotheram afferts, that one of the readieft and beft methods of filtering water, is, to let it run through a bed of clean fand. This is, he fays, preferable to the filtering-ftone, as it per⸳ forms its work much fooner; and the grains of fand are of fo many different figures, that they are pretty fure to ftop the progrefs of any bodies of fenfible bulk, in paffing through them §.

* Boerh. Chem. vol. 1. p. 348.

‡ M. Amy on Cifterns; but fee above, p. 31.

§ If you view ten thoufand grains of fand through a microfcope, you will fcarcely find two of the fame fize and fhape. Rotheram's Philofophical Inquiry, p. 48.

" A friend

" A friend of mine, fays the Doctor, in this town [Newcaftle] has a ciftern for collecting rain water, fo conftructed, that it both allows the water to fubfide, and the upper part of it to run through a bed of fand, which is raifed by a partition above the bottom of the ciftern; by which means the water becomes perfectly clear and bright, and is preferred by moft who have tafted it, to any other water in this town".

4. Some have objected, but probably without reafon, to this mode of filtration, on a prefumption, that the fand has the fame effect on the water as the filtering ftone : for it is faid, that the fand is infenfibly diffolved by the water ; fo that in four or five years it will have loft a fifth part of its weight. M. Amy therefore recommends the filtration of water through a fpunge, more or lefs compreffed. And this, he affures us, will render it, not only more clear, but more wholefome, than either a ftone or fand.

5. As the pureft of all water is obtained by diftillation, Dr. Heberden recommends this method, as particularly ufeful where fuel is cheap,

and

and the water is bad ; as it is in fome of our foreign fettlements.

The firft running of diftilled water has a difagreeable mufty tafte: on this account, if the ftill
hold twenty gallons, it will be neceffary to throw
away the firft gallon. The reft, through free
from this muftinefs, will have a difagreeable empyreumatic or burnt tafte. This tafte goes off by
keeping about a month, by ventillation, in a few
minutes, or by boiling the water in an open veffel. Diftilled water muft be kept in perfectly
clean glafs or ftone bottles, with glafs ftoppers,
or metal covers; and then, having in it no principle of corruption, it is incapable of being
fpoiled, and will keep juft the fame for ever.
But the leaft particle of any animal or vegetable
fubftance, will fpoil a great quantity ; and therefore the ftill and bottles fhould be kept wholly
for this ufe.

This procefs, though certainly attended with
many good effects, requires too much time and
attention for common ufe; and therefore, in general, it may be fufficient to adopt the mode
of

of filteration, recommended by Dr. Rotheram, or that which is propofed by M. Amy.

The obfervations, which I have here laid before the reader, are not new. They have been communicated to the public by others. But they are difperfed through many different publications. I have therefore thrown them into a fmall compafs. And I flatter myfelf, that, in this commodious form, they may be acceptable to the public; as many of the foregoing articles are of infinite importance to the health, and confequently to the happinefs of mankind.

F I N I S.